LADIES
OF THE
LAKE

A NOVEL BY

KEN
CORDAY

BEAUFORT
BOOKS

Library of Congress Cataloging-in-Publication Data available upon request

For inquiries about orders, please contact:
Beaufort Books
27 West 20th Street
Suite 1102
New York, NY 10011
sales@beaufortbooks.com

Published in the United States by Beaufort Books
www.beaufortbooks.com

Distributed by Midpoint Trade Books
www.midpointtrade.com

Printed in the United Staes of America

Corday, Ken
        Ladies of the Lake
        ISBN:
        Hardcover: 9780825307843
        eBook: 9780825307140

Design by Dick Roberts and David Pascal

CAST OF CHARACTERS

HUDSON AND VIVIAN MONTGOMERY
Their Daughter, CASSIDY

ALPHONSE AND ANGELICA LOUIS
Their Daughter, ALANA

SHERATON AND MORGAN FIRESTONE
Their Daughter, MADELYN ("MADDIE")
Their Son & Maddie's Half Brother, JAMES

JONATHAN AND CRYSTAL AMHURST

CARSON AND LISA ROTH
Their Children, WYATT, CHASE, and LIAM (Lisa's stepsons)

TOMMY AND DOROTHY NOLAN
Their Adopted Son, ZAC

LISA'S MOTHER
MARGARET CRANSTON

HUDSON'S MISTRESS
CLARA

THE DETECTIVE
SHAWN DANIELS

CASSIDY

May 31

1

"MY FATHER DECAPITATED HIMSELF LAST NIGHT."

I pulled a pack of Camel Pink #9's out of my Louis Vuitton and lit up, allowing time for the group to absorb my bombshell.

Zac was the first to regain speech. "He what? He chopped off his head?" Zac stared at me. Silence.

Alana took a strand of her long, chocolate-brown hair and twirled it around her finger. "Is he dead?"

These are my friends. For better or worse, in sickness and in health, till death do us part. We'd known each other since elementary school. We got braces at the same time, lost our virginities around the same time (not to each other), and did not want to be separated by geography during college, but were about to hit that age where we were going to have to cut the cord and go our own ways…and I couldn't bear the thought. They were the first voices I wanted to hear in the morning and the last before I went to sleep. Considering how rich and screwed up our parents were, we'd been through some fraught shit. Our folks' adulteries, addictions, divorces, indictments, and tabloid headlines had turned us into bitter and cynical teenagers. But this was a whole new level of shit. I took a puff and looked around. What a sight the five of us made. Body image is super important. Exotic half-Hispanic Alana, golden-haired cheerleader Maddie, and I had been doing yoga since preschool and started a strict regimen of Atkins when we turned twelve. And the guys, Zac and James, started mixing anabolic steroids into their Wheaties around the time they started playing with Legos. Our mothers paid very little attention to us except when it came to sun exposure and second-hand smoke…which is funny now, because we all smoke. But we never got into the tanning thing, having learned to apply about five layers of SPF 50 every time we went to Maui.

So I look at us now and think…holy crap…starved, pale, hung-over. If someone came in looking to cast a teenage vampire movie, they would have hit the mother lode with us.

At the moment of my entrance, Zac was sitting on the pool table rubbing the buzz cut he'd just gotten to his black hair. He'd had hippie-style long hair forever so the new look hadn't grown on me—or him—yet. James was also sitting on the pool table, rolling the balls around randomly and sipping on a beer. We sometimes teased him, calling him Hawk, because he refused to change the Mohawk hairstyle that he'd had for about three years, which looked ridiculous.

The club's recreational room was down the hall from the dining room, and wasn't open for brunch yet, but it would be soon. I could hear clanking sounds coming from the kitchen. I figured we had ten minutes before we got kicked out. Madelyn was splitting her half-brother James' beer as she laid on the floor underneath the table. He'd pass it to her and she'd pass it back. They were both majorly hung over and enjoying a little "hair of the dog." It had been a helluva party last night. Some bullshit charity gig my mom threw to raise money for…for… um…damn. What with all the head severing going on, I'd forgotten the point of last night's *gala-grand-event*. (I put that last part in italics so you'd recognize the sarcasm.) A janitor guy was vacuuming and window washers were doing their thing, but no one dared kicked us out. Emron would. He was the club manager. But he hadn't put in an appearance. So the mood remained chill between the five of us. Shocked, but chill. We were all still hurting from last night. The country club staff was trying to work around us. I'm sure they heard everything we said, but I didn't give a damn.

Zac, Madelyn, Alana, James, and I were all club babies. That's what the staff called us behind our backs. They thought we were lame, rich, entitled, spoiled, and irresponsible. Like those are bad things. What they didn't appreciate about us was our intense loyalty. That didn't mean we didn't get on each other's nerves occasionally. All eyes switched from me to Alana who jumped up from her cushy armchair and raced over to me: "Is he okay? I mean, did he survive?"

I said, "Sure, Lan…Dad's doing just fine without his head. In fact, he's pouring orange juice and coffee down his neck right now."

James slapped Alana on the arm. "You idiot. Of course he's dead."

Maddie took off her sunglasses and I could see her eyes, bulging, blinking. I think she was having some sort of aneurysm, although sixteen is a little young for that. She tried to swallow and talk at the same time. The result was her beer spewing over all of us. She choked out, "I mean…about an hour ago…at my house…we were just talking about all the sirens last night. It was super annoying. But all of us were…well, my whole family had been too boiled to check it out. We just kind of stayed passed out through it all."

Alana didn't remember sirens. "The police were at your house, Cass?"

Zac's tone was one of disgust. "Of course the police came. Cassidy's mom had a headless cadaver on her hands. Also, I'm sure the coroner was there and an ambulance and…"

"Yeah, lots of that sort of thing." I took a deep puff, fully aware I was in the middle of the most bizarre conversation I'd ever had. Or ever would have. I hope.

Maddie offered me the rest of her beer. I squelched down my lifelong fear of backwash and drank it. Then I looked at Zac. He was going to need details. And here it came…the onslaught of endless questions.

I threw myself on the floor and stared at the ceiling. I'd always hated this clubhouse room. There was too much red wallpaper and rustic furniture and the chandeliers were made out of what looked like fake deer antlers. All the rooms looked this way at the club. But for better or worse, this was our home away from home. It did have a nice glass window overlooking the pool, patio bar, and eighteenth green.

I took another sip and a deep breath. All three were hurling questions at me.

"Shut up and listen! Dad just backed up his convertible out of the garage, top down, and the door sliced off his head."

Zac jumped off the table and got in my face. "Was he that drunk? Just a stupid accident? How slow does your garage door open anyway?"

"I haven't timed it lately."

Alana shook her head in disbelief. "I just saw him last night. Here. He danced with my mom. My mom," she repeated, as if that were some sort of significant piece of evidence. Then a light bulb went off over her head. "Hey, spending any time with my mom makes me want to kill myself. Do you think?"

I took another long drag. "There is some talk of suicide, but that's an impossible way to kill yourself. I mean who would do that? He and my stepmom were arguing and I'm sure he wanted to silence the sound of her nagging, but to purposefully lop off his head? I don't think so. Anyway, even if it was some drunken form of suicide, I don't think doing the cha-cha with your mom pushed my dad over the edge, Lan."

James leaned in, "But how could it have just been an accident? I've seen your dad wasted a million times. That guy could hold his liquor. There's no way he could have been that stupid. Your dad was a cool guy. He seemed to have an okay time last night. And now? It's crazy. We need answers."

"Damn, you guys are worse than the police. I don't have any answers. Yeah. He was here all smiles and playing the part of charitable host. He and my stepmom chaired the party. Remember? My dad gave a speech."

James threw the cue ball in the side pocket. "No, we don't remember because we were all getting stoned behind the kitchen."

I sighed. "That's right. Well, anyway, they raised like a bazillion bucks for…for…Oh, now I remember…starving and abandoned children in Africa. I guess the police haven't ruled out some insane moment of suicidal thoughts. They kept asking me all sorts of jack-ass questions like if I'd sensed any depression in my dad or if I knew of any financial setback he might have just suffered. I said no and no. I was still pretty wasted. I don't remember most of the questions. I'm sure I'll have to go through it all again—only sober next time. They also asked me if there had been any tension between my dad and stepmom. I needed clarification on that question and joked, 'You mean last night, or for the last three years?' Cops have no sense of humor."

The brunch staff was starting to pour in. No one checked ID cards with us, and it wasn't tough to get a Bloody Mary. I drank it down in two gulps, licked off the salt, and took another puff.

James jumped up, grabbed a pool cue, and twirled it like a baton. "This is huge. What led up to the whole lop-off? Start from what happened when your folks got home."

"I don't remember much. At the end of the party, my stepmom was pissed that I was high and had been grinding on the dance floor with Zac. She threw me in the car and she and my dad took me home. I went to bed and tried to sleep. Downstairs Dad and Viv were really going at each other, screaming, yelling, name calling, a usual Saturday night at our house.

"Finally dehydration got the better of me, and I went to get some water. When I got to the hallway the fight escalated. Name calling, threats, that sort of thing. I heard my dad say he was going out. Then, my stepmom shrieked at him in that horrible high-pitched voice that only dogs can hear. I went downstairs. Even though I was still wasted, I thought I could play referee. I found them in the garage. Dad compacted his six-foot-four frame into his BMW and opened the top. It's all kind of a blur after that. He hit the button on his visor to open the garage door. Viv hit the one near the door to the house to close it. I thought,

Holy Jesus Christ, these two are acting like five-year-olds. Dad eventually won the battle of the buttons and floored the car backwards. I don't know what happened…I mean, what made it happen. But the garage door only went halfway up. I kind of remember Dad's head being torn off his body, and I kind of still think it was just a bad dream. Vivian screamed. Then she saw me and grabbed me, and the next thing I knew I was in my bed again. I must have passed out, but even in my coma-like state, I could sort of hear sirens, but like they were far away instead of right in front of my house. I must have been in shock. That, combined with the weed and the alcohol, knocked me out."

Maddie and Alana were unspooling. Maddie was the worst. She actually grabbed me by the arms and started to shake me.

"How could you just go back to bed? I mean your house was swarming with all these first response guys. Obviously, the walls of the garage must have been covered in blood and brain stuff."

Zac was sidetracked. "First response? Where'd you ever hear that term? Did you actually pay attention to that movie they showed us at school about 9/11?"

Maddie grabbed my cigarette out of my hand and threw it on the ground. "Cassidy Montgomery, tell us what happened next?"

I continued, "Right or wrong, I was so stoned and out of it, I stumbled back to bed. Then, a couple of hours later, my stepmom woke me up. Her face was all streaked with makeup. She looked like a zombie.

"She told me to get up, that it was time to emotionally grapple with what had happened the night before. Grapple. She actually used that word. I was ordered to get up, get some coffee in me, and she'd tell me everything.

"So I followed her to the kitchen. My mouth was still so dry I could barely open it. There was police tape across the door from the kitchen to the garage, and there were three guys taking pictures, writing things down…I didn't really pay much attention.

"I saw a venti latte on the counter with my name on it. And that's when I had my first cogent thought of the day. Who the hell had gone out in the middle of all this and gotten me Starbucks? Seriously. Despite the cops and the sirens and the warnings and the yellow tape, it was the Starbucks cup that really got my attention. It wasn't very hot, but I drank it and it helped me focus. My stepmom kept looking at my face… studying it. Unnerving. You know how she has that pinched nose and those beady eyes? Well, she looked more like a ferret than ever. Her hair was matted and her sweat clothes were stained with—I don't know what. Maybe tea. She's always drinking tea like she's the fucking Queen of England. It was freakish how she stared at me, obviously waiting for a sign that I was mentally all there. Then, when she saw the caffeine kick in, I was accosted by some cop. He asked me questions I didn't have the answers to. I just wanted to go back to bed."

I looked at my four best friends, one by one. I studied their faces. The story I'd just told them was certainly a level ten on the bizarre scale, and it had cleared away all the fog from their brains. They were right in the moment with me. And they totally had my back.

It was group hug time, which I allowed for about fifteen seconds before I pulled away.

Maddie couldn't believe it. "You're not crying or freaking out or anything. You loved your dad. I know you did. You were his princess."

Alana concurred, "Yeah, ever since I've known you, which has been like, since the second grade, you and your dad have been so tight. Even when he divorced your bitch of a mom and he married Vivian, you and he were so there for each other. And now he's dead. I'm so sorry."

Zac put his arm around me. "I know you're done with the hug thing, but we're here for you."

"Totally." James was ready to get me another drink, but I batted his hand down when he tried to get the passing waiter's attention.

"I'm fine. I just need some time. Just let me process, okay?"

Process. They nodded. We'd all been to therapy at various times in our lives and that was a word they knew well. It made them feel safe… like they were sure I was using my coping tools.

Zac looked at his watch. "Shit. I have to go."

He kissed me on the forehead. "I'll come over to your place later." And he was gone.

The others had places to be, nails to get polished, spin classes to take, but they all assured me they'd be there for me through the whole ordeal to come. My dad's body was somewhere in a morgue, and his head was not on top of it. I wasn't sure what "ordeal" in the future they were talking about. I guess the funeral. Damn. I hadn't even thought about the funeral.

I could see it now. My four best buddies, dressed in their newest outfits from their favorite fashion websites, holding my hand. They'd be there for me then. In the church, at the graveside, and all the days to follow. I knew they would. But now they were gone and I was glad. I was finally alone. Even the waiters steered clear of me as I sat on top of the pool table and closed my eyes.

Slowly one tear started to fall. Then another.

Despite the fact that I had been doing my best to push down any memories of my father, now that I was alone, they rose to the surface one at a time. My dad picking me up and throwing me in the waves in the ocean when I was about nine. Midnight ice cream snacks and watching *The Wizard of Oz* or *Parent Trap* or *Harry Potter*, bonding over the fact we were both terrible insomniacs. In seventh grade, I hid my report card from him, forged his name, and sent it back in. Of course, the forgery looked terrible, and he was called into the principal's office. This was after my mom died and before he'd married Vivian, so he was all the parent I had. He wrapped his arms around me and told me he knew I wasn't a dishonest person. So what was going on? I was embarrassed and frustrated. I'd gotten an F in math. It had always been my dream to work with my dad at his computer hardware company. But how could I do that if I was a math idiot? He laughed and held me and told me not to worry. He knew just what to do.

The next day he took me to a board meeting. Boy was I bored. After that I wanted nothing to do with making computer chips, and that was just fine with Dad. Sure, there were lots of terrible times. He wasn't the best dad in the world. But those tender, amazing moments overwhelmed me. The dam burst. I started sobbing and shouting every horrible, nasty expletive I could think of. I threw the empty Bloody Mary glass through the window of the clubhouse and ran outside. I stopped on the practice green, pulled the flag out of the hole in the turf and started jamming the bottom of the stick into my thighs, my arms, my neck, then threw it into the window of the clubhouse. Glass went flying…some of it into my face and arms. But I didn't care. I sat on the ground sobbing and bleeding. And then I think I passed out. Considering the circumstances, it seemed appropriate.

2

I WOKE UP BACK IN BED. I went to rub my neck and realized I had a bandage on my arm. I felt around. Bandages, tape, all over me. I turned my head. My stepmom was hovering over me, rubbing her hands against her thighs and fighting tears.

"Oh, you're awake. I'm so sorry. I never should have let you leave the house."

"It's alright. I'm fine now."

I could hear whispered voices downstairs. Viv's posse was here. Some of the women were moms or stepmoms of my friends. All were members of the club and had been at the party last night. Their gated housing community consisted of mansions which encircled a man-made lake. And Vivian's besties occupied several of them. Their nickname was "The Ladies of the Lake." Tommy (Zac's dad) had used the moniker as a kind of an insult. The Ladies of the Lake sounded lofty, deriving its name from either British Folklore or a Raymond Chandler novel. Tommy thought he was being very funny. These women had not stepped out of folklore or a classy who-dun-it from the '40s. They lived only to gossip, shop, and spend their husbands' money. On the surface they seemed to care only about status. But underneath...well, there was something there. None of these women had grown up rich. They were strong. But they hid their strength under their Valentino ready-to-wear. People tried to tease them now and again, but they didn't seem to mind the nickname. Anyway, they were all in my living room. Shit.

"Vivian, please tell your friends to go home. We don't need them here."

"It's times like this we need our friends the most. They're so upset about what happened to your dad, and they just want to support us. Doctor Lazare was here earlier. He's the one who patched you up. He left a mild sedative. Want to take it?"

"Sure." I downed the pill quickly without water.

"Hurting yourself is not the best way to handle your grief."

"Really? What is the best way?"

"We'll see a grief counselor together tomorrow. In the meantime just rest."

Viv left the room. I waited a few minutes for the pill to kick in. Nothing. My system is pretty used to drugs of almost any kind so a one-milligram Xanax or whatever it was wasn't going to hit the spot. It was okay. I didn't really want to zonk out. I was still "processing."

I got out of bed. Ouch. I really did bang myself up. Trying to ignore the pain, I made my way to the top of the stairs, then halfway down to the landing where I could peek into the living room. Sure enough they were all there—my stepmom's cronies.

Clearly in charge of the newly formed grief committee was Maddie's mom, Morgan. There were three other women huddled around Viv, but Morgan was the most aggressive, trying to get my stepmom to put her feet up, drink some herbal tea, stuff like that. Vivian pushed the tea away and refused to lie down. I'm not a huge fan of my father's second wife, but I have to say she held up pretty well. I strained to listen…

"I couldn't possibly rest. I have to focus on Cassidy. She's clearly out of her mind. And why wouldn't she be."

Alana's mom, Angelica Louis, hovered on the periphery. She clearly felt uncomfortable and looked like she wanted to bolt. Being caring and sympathetic were not qualities she possessed. I knew she was just hanging around because her absence would speak volumes about her lack of loyalty to the group. While the other women's appearances were in various stages of disarray…hastily thrown-on couture sweat suits, yoga pants and the like, Angelica was perfectly put together. I noticed she'd taken the time to coif her long, black hair into a bun at the top of her head. Her hair and makeup were flawless, and she was wearing Chanel from head to toe. After hearing the horror story about my dad's accident, she obviously didn't rush over. Not till she looked perfect.

Crystal Amhurst was manning the phone, which rang every few minutes. She'd listen for a moment, then tersely respond, "No comment," and hang up. Finally, she just unplugged the damn thing. Then she went to my stepmom's purse and took out her cell.

"I'm turning this off, Viv. The press are hounding you for a statement. You need to be shielded."

"Thanks, Crystal. You're such a good friend. You're all so wonderful. Considering what's happened, I wouldn't be surprised if you never said a word to me again."

At thirty-two years old, Crystal was the youngest of the group and its newest member. She had only been married to her husband, Jonathan, for two years. But everyone knew the union was already on the rocks.

Crystal desperately wanted to get pregnant. Her husband had a grown daughter from a previous marriage. Jonathan was quite a bit older than Crystal. In fact, his daughter and his new wife were about the same age. Jonathan was rich…probably the richest of our rich little fellowship. He was used to having his way. Crystal was always on eggshells with Jonathan. While she was certainly the perfect example of a trophy wife, she knew her looks weren't going to be enough to keep Jonathan happy. She was desperate to give him the one thing he didn't have…a son.

I knew, as everyone in their inner circle seemed to, that Crystal had gone through a series of fertility treatments, which so far, had proved unsuccessful. The more time passed, the more days and weeks Jonathan stayed away. I don't know much about infertility, but I do know that you can't make a baby if the potential daddy isn't around much.

I had never liked Jonathan, even though he was Dad's friend. He flaunted his wealth and his power. But I did have a soft place in my heart for poor Crystal, sentiments that were strengthened by the protective way Crystal acted during this surreal morning after.

Lisa Roth, the wife of Carson, one of the most powerful talent agents in Hollywood, came over to sit next to Vivian and pat her hand in the most patronizingly cliché act of sympathy I had ever seen. I took another step down so I could hear what was being spoken in the most hushed of tones.

Lisa hated to be practical but didn't they have to think about Hudson's business? And his will?

A strong voice with a flat, New York accent could be heard from the marbled entryway. "Why didn't anyone tell me about Hudson? Why did I have to hear about it on Good Morning America? I mean, am I not a part of this community?"

I moved back quickly up to the landing. I didn't need to strain to hear that voice. It was Dorothy Nolan. Dorothy was originally from Brooklyn and spent most of her adult life as a pole dancer and "paid escort." There wasn't much to her story. Her husband, on the other hand, had a very interesting past.

Tommy climbed the ranks of the world's golf elite in the 1970's. After placing fourth in the U.S. Open, he rose to the rank of seventh in the nation. He had just started to get the really great spokesperson deals with various sporting goods manufacturers, cereal makers, and soda companies, when he suddenly retired amidst some sort of gambling scandal.

He married his then-prostitute girlfriend, Dorothy, and worked through a string of club pro jobs, eventually landing him here in Avalon.

Dorothy and Tommy never took enough time off from their careers to have kids, so by the time they retired and got around to starting a family, it was too late to go the biological route. So they adopted Zac when he had just turned twelve. Until then, Zac had gone from foster home to foster home. He behaved for the Nolans, glad to have a permanent family, but he'd had a tough transition, going from broken and living in the east side of L.A. to the lush life Tommy and Dotty could afford him. I think that's why I always liked Zac the best. He was cool and wasn't totally into the money and the stuff, and he was also loyal to his adoptive mom and dad, who could, at times, be a little embarrassing.

Dorothy and Tommy tried to fit in. Tommy was sort of a mascot of the men of the club. He was fun to have around, with his flowing white hair and his year-round tan, but he always needed to borrow money. Dotty tried to hide the fact that they were always low on funds, but she was smart and she knew she wasn't as polished as the other Ladies, and the other women could never quite forget Dotty's scandalous past. However, Dorothy plunged ahead, determined to make a place for herself and her family inside the club's inner group. The other Ladies were still too dazed or upset to protest as "Dot" headed for the kitchen proclaiming that what this family needed was a big bowl of her homemade chicken soup. I had to laugh to myself despite the situation. An ex-whore's chicken soup that had come out of a can. I slipped back inside my bedroom and downed another pill before I was forced to endure an actual encroachment of one of the Ladies. Dotty had no personal boundaries, and I knew she'd come barging into my room in about twenty minutes with some broth and lots of unsolicited advice. Fortunately, by the time the soup was ready, I was fast asleep.

When I woke up, I could hear that all my stepmom's friends were still there. Damnit. Wasn't there anything like privacy anymore? Then my ears perked up as I heard a man's voice. This I had to see for myself... some testosterone had barged its way into the sea of estrogen.

I made my way back down to the landing. I could see him. Damn, he was all kinds of good looking. From the way he was questioning the women, I could tell he was a cop. I picked up on Lisa calling him Detective Daniels.

None of the women seemed upset by his presence or his questions. Maybe that's because he seemed so relaxed. He assured them over and over that this was just a routine follow-up, and he'd be out of their hair in a moment.

I took two more steps down the stairs so I could see better, and what I saw is the stuff movies are made of. The detective turned to ask Crystal a question. He must not have noticed her before, because the minute he set eyes on her he started to stammer. He worked hard to regain his composure, but it was clear that her beauty had a powerful effect on him. And Crystal responded with her own coy brand of shyness.

Suddenly it seemed like these were the only two in the room. For a moment, all talking had ceased and there was just the eye lock between Daniels and Crystal and silence.

Then, the silence became uncomfortable because everyone started talking at once. The detective closed his notebook and told the gals he had all the information he needed, but he might be back to tie up a few loose ends. That statement was easily translated into a clear observation that he was looking for any excuse to see Crystal again. The fact that she was married seemed to be lost on both of them.

I went back to bed, and my thoughts wandered from the fraught moment between Crystal and the police guy to my dad being dead… gone forever. I took another pill. I couldn't handle all the feelings bombarding me at once. I needed to shut down. And despite the fact that all I had to look forward to was the horrible event of my father's funeral, the meds did their trick and for a while, I slept more and didn't have to think about it.

3

IT WAS AN OPEN CASKET SERVICE.

"You've got to be fucking kidding me," I whispered to Zac.

"Did they sew his head back on?" Alana was more intrigued than repulsed.

"I don't know, but I'm not going to look," whispered Madelyn.

"I need a drink." Alana didn't handle stress very well.

"Well, you should have thought of that before we left. There will be plenty of booze at the party afterwards. Just live in the world of the sober for an hour or so." James was the only one who could calm Alana down when she got like this.

Alana had been diagnosed with ADHD a year before. She swore to her parents that she was taking her meds, but her friends knew differently. The meds didn't mix well with booze and Alana wasn't about to give up her favorite pastime, no matter what the docs said. So, she saved the Adderall for her friends and self-medicated with alcohol. None of us blamed her. There was an inbred distrust of all adults that ran rampant through the whole younger generation.

Trepidation. That was the only word that came to my mind as we walked into the chapel. I thought of another appropriate word—dread. The air in the chapel almost felt heavy with it. We slowly walked down the aisle. The black and gold ornate coffin was surrounded by an entire hothouse of flowers and a giant photo of Hudson.

Careful to avert my eyes away from the casket, I stepped up and touched the photo. I'd always thought my dad was the most handsome man in the world. I loved him so much and he knew it. We'd been through so much…the dissolution of his marriage to my mom. Then when my mom died of cancer, my dad paid for everything, even though he'd moved on to Vivian. It was rotten timing for me having just turned the tender age of thirteen. I wanted to hate Vivian, and I wanted to hate Dad. And I did for a while. All those good memories from my early childhood had been erased.

Then, Dad took me out of school and flew me up to Alaska. He rented a yacht for just the two of us and we spent a week floating on the ocean, weaving through icebergs. At night, Dad would tell the captain to cut the engines. It was so silent. The stars looked so close. Giant mountains of icebergs passed us by. I felt small in such a big universe that didn't seem to care about the designer name on your shoes, or the color of pill you took, or the year on the label of your bottle of wine.

We talked about deep stuff. I don't remember most of it. What I did hold close in my heart was that I was Dad's number one priority that week. I thought of that trip now as I looked at Dad's face. The photo caught his spirit, the light in his eyes, the hunger for life to do everything bigger and better. That hunger had made him a millionaire. That same hunger had kept him at the office late most nights, away many weekends. The trip to Alaska was the last time I'd had any one-on-one time with him. We grew apart. He sort of changed, became distant. He started kind of ignoring me. I didn't feel like his princess anymore. We had become strangers to each other. He could actually be cruel on occasion, bad-mouthing everything—the club, my friends, my schoolwork (which was not bad). Lately, he had seemed discontented and irritable all the time. And he saved his worst barbs for Vivian. I'm no fan of the woman, but I did feel sorry for the way he talked to her. Though Vivian had been a prominent scientist before she gave it all up and married my dad, he treated her like yesterday's trash. I don't know how she put up with it.

I saw my stepmom alone in the front row. Vivian saw me, patted the seat next to her as an invitation for me to sit with her. But I just couldn't. Vivian wasn't family. She was surrounded by her real family, the Ladies of the Lake and their husbands. Alphonse and Anjelica Louis, Sheraton and Morgan Firestone, Jonathan and Crystal Amhurst, Carson and Lisa Roth, and last and certainly least, Dorothy and Tommy Nolan.

My friends decided to form a clan of our own…a united front. They put me in the middle of the third row and slid in on each side of me as if they could protect me from the grief that washed over me.

I could see the seating arrangement hurt Vivian's feelings, but that was not my problem. The room was filled with the rich and famous, all there to pay their respects to a public figure. But the whispered comments that I could easily hear were far from respectful. It was how Dad died and not the fact that he was dead that was the topic of the moment…a moment that should have been filled with talk of his wit, his intelligence, and his ambition. Instead, there was speculation about the garage door, the horrible way he died, and curiosity about the appearance of the coffin. Everyone was at a loss as to why the coffin was open, though no one had dared look in.

I would have bolted out of there but Zac sensed my panic and gently took my hand. His touch stilled my thoughts. The minister began the service, and he said all the things that everyone should have been thinking…wonderful things about Dad. Then, Alphonse spoke briefly about his golfing buddy, trying in vain to lighten the mood with stories of Hudson's ongoing battle with a certain sand trap on the eighth hole. Alphonse was an actor so, of course, his eulogy was clever and engaging. He loved being the center of attention, even here at his best friend's funeral.

Alphonse was a classically trained Welsh actor who never seemed to get his big break. While he watched contemporaries, Bruce Willis and Tom Hanks, rise to stardom, for decades, he had to be satisfied playing many supporting roles, including widely popular two-dimensional romantic leads, eventually settling for a series of butlers, chauffeurs, and bumbling sidekicks in both British and American movies. I never really liked being around him, because he was always bragging about some movie he was doing or some award he was up for. I already told you what I thought of his ice cube of a wife, Anjelica, who had been born and raised in Mexico. How they produced such an amazing daughter as Alana, I'll never know. When Alphonse finished, I reached over and squeezed Alana's hand and whispered, "Your dad did a nice job." She just shrugged. She didn't care for her father any more than I did.

I actually emitted a sigh of frustration when Jonathan got up to speak. I didn't mean for it to be so loud, but seriously? Jonathan? He and Dad played golf together but were not that great of friends. Why was he talking?

Not being the natural speaker that Alphonse was, Jonathan fumbled a little. Still, I had to admit he was a good-looking guy, especially for being as old as he was. He had to be in his mid-sixties.

As I was staring at him now, I saw everything about him was fake. His nose, his hair plugs, his tan, his teeth. He didn't have a job. Jonathan had inherited most of the real estate along the Wilshire Boulevard corridor to the east of the 405 freeway. The rental checks just kept coming in, and Jonathan kept cashing them. He'd been married before to some Pasadena debutante, and they had a daughter named Jessica. Jess married a guy named Charles, and they lived off of Jonathan's money. They had a baby girl so Jonathan was a grandfather. Still he wanted a son. As I said before, his wife, Crystal, idolized him and was doing everything she could to give him one. But, as I said before, that wasn't going so well.

Jonathan also spoke about what a great businessman Dad was, but how he never made money at the expense of others. The moment was uncomfortable, as if Jonathan wanted to confess that Hudson had all the class that Jonathan lacked. But he stopped short of admitting that he himself was an asshole.

Tommy was too choked up to speak. His pain touched me so much. Tommy, for all his silly behavior and flakey antics, was a tender-hearted person. The death of his dear friend, Hudson, was too much. Dotty clung to her husband who just couldn't find the strength to stand up and speak.

Carson was next. He eulogized his friend as a man who loved his wife and daughter. His speech was short and sweet, and he ended it by going to Vivian and then me and giving us hugs. Carson was a man full of energy and emotion. He was one of the biggest talent agents in Hollywood. Everyone was his buddy, and his specialty was taking on high maintenance clients. The kind that were always getting DUI's and arrested for tearing up hotel rooms. There was something about Carson…I couldn't put my finger on it…something slimy. But he was always nice to me. Lisa was his fourth wife. He had three kids from his three previous wives. None of the biological moms wanted to raise their own brats so Carson usually had all his kids staying with him, which meant Lisa was in charge of fifteen-year-old Wyatt, twelve-year-old Chase, and nine-year-old Liam. They were a handful. I did not envy Lisa's life. Lisa was an okay lady. I often wondered why she put up with the craziness of Carson and his drunken clients and the bratty kids. But she did. If she resented it or hated it in any way, she never showed it. Either she was a brilliant faker or a martyr.

I was afraid Sheraton was going to speak. I think Maddie was afraid her dad was going to talk too, but he didn't. His wife, Morgan, seemed relieved as well. Sheraton was really only interested in talking about one thing…himself. There was quite a bit of gossip at the club as to who was really richer, Sheraton or Jonathan. Unlike Jonathan, Sheraton earned his money. He owned a vast fleet of luxury cruise liners. He also owned a commercial garage full of collectible cars. And he didn't have them up on blocks. He drove them. He loved to show them off. He adored flaunting his wealth. Actually, his wife, Morgan, did too. Jonathan was hardly ever home, needing to constantly supervise his fleet of ships. He bragged that he was a very "hands on" guy. That suited Morgan just fine. Maddie knew her parents barely tolerated each other. She'd often confided in me that she never understood why they even stayed together. Maybe their mutual love of material possessions bonded them. It sure wasn't Maddie. She had been raised by a series of nannies since the moment she was born. In fact, if Maddie didn't have us for friends, she would have been all alone in the world. Basically, the teenagers sitting in this pew with her…we were her family.

But today was not about Maddie, it was about me. I forced my face to remain frozen, expressionless. Besides that one sigh, I had remained silent. I would behave. I wouldn't besmirch the memory of my father. I would shake everyone's hand and thank them for attending. But I wasn't going to mean a word of it. This was all a sham.

There was an audible gasp of relief when the ceremony came to an end. Alphonse, Carson, Tommy, Jonathan, and Sheraton were among the pallbearers. The casket was closed and taken down the road to the burial site. I followed behind with the rest. The center aisle of the chapel jammed up quickly, no one could get out fast enough. The country club was the chosen site of the reception, and everyone was anxious to get my father's body to his final resting place, then get a cocktail or two under their belts.

I watched my dad's closest friends carry him to the burial spot…a prominent location right outside the chapel. We stood around the gaping hole in the ground. Someone laid an elaborate display of flowers on top of the black coffin.

The minister read a final passage from the Bible, and a final prayer was offered.

When it was all over, Vivian and I were swamped by people wanting to offer their condolences. Both Vivian and I gently pushed our friends away, promising we'd meet up again at the club. We just needed a moment.

When we were alone, I confronted Vivian. "An open casket? What the hell were you thinking?"

"I couldn't bear to put him into the ground like…that. I spent a fortune on finding the best person in the world who could…make him whole again. But not one of our friends had the guts to look."

"I'll look," I said. I walked to the casket, which had not yet been placed in the ground. I pulled off the ornate flower arrangement on top of it and strained to lift the lid. My actions were insane but all our friends had already gone inside, and there was no one but Vivian to stop me.

I looked down at my father who so looked not dead…just like he was taking a very long nap. Viv must have hired a miracle worker or something because he looked completely intact.

I turned to my stepmom and hugged her, "You did a great job. I'm sorry you went to all that trouble and no one saw how wonderful he looks."

Vivian was as startled as I by the hug but clung to me. "You seeing him made it all worthwhile."

It was the first nice moment Vivian and I had ever had and it was short-lived. I pulled back, "If you and Dad hadn't been screaming at each other in the first place…if he hadn't been so desperate to get away from you, this wouldn't have happened."

Vivian didn't put up a fight. Instead, she said the strangest thing imaginable. "I know." And she walked out leaving me with my dead father, a look of shock on my face.

4

THE NEXT MORNING, I STUMBLED DOWN for coffee to find my stepmother sipping her cup of tea and pretending to read the morning paper.

"Maybe you should take some of the pills the doc gave me. You look like you're about to explode."

Vivian's answer was brittle, "I don't need pharmaceuticals. I'll be more relaxed after we get this damned ordeal over."

I poured my coffee. "There's more ordeal to come? Seriously? Isn't this family ordealed out?"

"Why do you have to have your father's lack of empathy?"

"Must be something about the gene pool."

Vivian sighed, then got up from the table and came and knelt near my kitchen chair. Not so sure I was comfortable with her breaking my personal bubble space. Also, I was a little on the shocked side that she'd risk wrinkles in her linen skirt. But the look in her eyes was serious. She had worn glasses before she married Dad, but he made her get contacts. Trust me. That didn't help. Of all the Ladies of the Lake, she was the least physically appealing.

"Why did your father marry me?"

I choked on my coffee. "What?"

"Why did he marry me? It certainly wasn't for my looks. It wasn't for my smarts. He had access to all I had to offer the company when I was running his R and D division. That first night he asked me out, I was stunned and so nervous. I felt like a wallflower going out with a prince. I'm a practical woman but your dad was so kind to me that night…treated me like a queen that, for once, I felt like a woman."

"What had you been before then?"

"Please don't use that smart mouth with me. This is very important. He didn't love me. We didn't even make love on our wedding night. And in bed, well, I never seemed to make him happy. But I never gave up. I quit work. I took care of you full time, made his house, his life as beautiful as possible. No man had ever given me a second glance before. And here was the most handsome, successful man I knew, and he was my husband.

"You don't know how hard it is to be, well…you're so beautiful. I grew up feeling so unloved. So I resolved that I didn't need to be loved. My value would be in what my mind could achieve. I had just gotten to the place in my life where I was okay with that.

"Then Hudson swooped in. And the next thing I knew, it was designer dresses, private jets to Paris, having my hair and makeup done for me, and I felt cherished.

"Then we were married and the fairy tale was over. But I never gave up on him. Even in that garage. I was sure I could keep him. He was everything to me. He'd made me who I was. Without him…I'd be the nothing I'd always been."

I threw my cup into the sink. "This is way too much information. I don't know why Dad married you. I was as shocked as everyone else. What difference does it make now?"

Vivian stood up and almost shouted, "It makes all the difference in the world." Then she closed her eyes and gathered herself. "I'm sorry. This is not your burden. Excuse me. I have to go. Your father's will is being read today. You really should be there."

"No thanks." I was not the least bit interested. I was sure I'd get enough of a bundle to get away from this hag in three months when I turned eighteen. I ran upstairs and threw myself under the covers. I wanted to sleep until it was time to go to college.

⁂

"This is a private meeting," exclaimed Byron Jaztim, Hudson's lawyer. He was astonished to see Vivian and me enter his office with practically an entourage.

Okay, I was there, but only because Viv had dragged me out of bed. By way of protest, I was still in my pajamas, a fact that mortified my stepmother and which actually almost made the outing worth it. Besides, who would notice me? Viv had brought Crystal, Lisa, Dotty, Morgan, and Anjelica with her. Hail, hail, the gang's all here. This was the big moment. It was all about money. They weren't about to miss this.

Vivian took control of the meeting and intimidated the lawyer right behind his desk. She made the introductions quickly, insisting that her support system remain throughout the reading of the will.

Bryon got paid no matter who was in the room. He shrugged his shoulders and proceeded. "Very well."

Vivian sat as Byron's secretary scrambled to find chairs for Anjelica, Morgan, Crystal, Lisa, and Dot. I declined, preferring to stand in the corner. I didn't want anything to do with any of this. I wanted out of there. I didn't want Dad's money. As flawed and as mean as he often was, I just wanted him back.

Byron opened the file. I felt my knees start to buckle. "I'm outta here." I started to split.

Vivian followed me to the doorway. "You can't leave. You are your father's sole heir. He was the CEO of one of the largest computer hardware manufacturers in the world. Don't you want to hear what you'll get?"

"You make it sound like Wheel of Fortune or something. The money…the stuff…it's all got blood on it. Dad's blood. He was supposed to live for a long time. He was too young…I mean…It's all so…" I didn't know what to say. Damn. Tears were coming and I was not about to let Viv see me cry. I steeled myself. "I didn't win a prize, I lost my dad. And he was more than just numbers in a computer bank to me. You vultures want to peck over his carcass, fine. He's lost to me. And no amount of money can bring him back. So what's the point? You can all go to hell."

I ran. No one followed me.

⁊ₑ

The house was empty. I paced back and forth in front of the kitchen door which led to the garage. I hadn't been in there since…well, since.

I finally opened the door and went inside, flicked on the light. Dad's silver Mercedes was there, as was the black Porsche Carrera. I made my way to the empty spot of the garage.

For a rich guy, my dad was not the most organized or the neatest. There were toolboxes galore, filled with tools my dad never used, since he had a favorite mechanic on retainer. There were expensive mountain bikes, and even more expensive road bikes leaning up against the wall. Fishing rods, golf clubs, scuba gear…all kinds of crap. Dad was the outdoorsy type.

I forced myself to stand right where the BMW had been parked. I looked around. There were spots of oil, dirt, and dust all over the garage, but not where the Beemer had been. The police had been over that part of the garage with a fine-tooth comb. Not a spider web in the corner…nothing. Even more unnerving was that there was no sign of the accident. I knelt down and rubbed my hand against the floor. Not a shred of glass. I looked closer. Not a drop of blood. I closed my eyes. I thought back to that moment—my dad hauling ass out of the garage, the door half open, his head being torn from his neck. I opened my eyes and walked to the button on the wall next to the kitchen door. I touched it. The sound of the garage door opening startled me. It certainly didn't fly open, but it wasn't slow. How was it possible that my dad backed into it so fast? He'd been in and out of that garage hundreds of times. I sank to my knees. I wanted to cry again. It felt so good the first time. But I just couldn't. There were no tears now, just sorrow.

I heard a sound. I looked up and saw my four best friends coming up the driveway. Zac reached me first. He sat down next to me. James too. Alana leaned over and stroked my hair.

Maddie looked around, "So this is where it all happened. Damn. You'd never know. You'd just never know."

"They're reading my dad's will now."

Alana shed the tears I couldn't. "I know. My mom's there."

"Mine too," said Maddie.

"All that money. I don't even know how much there is. As messed up as they were, I just want to go back and have things the way they were. I just want..." I couldn't finish the sentence. But they all knew what I was thinking.

Zac hugged me tighter. "Fuck the money."

Maddie couldn't keep her mouth shut, "Well, I don't think any of us have ever said that before."

And there, in that terrible place, where my father lost his life, I found myself laughing for the first time in a long time.

5

"LOOK AT THIS ONE," VIVIAN PUSHED an envelope toward me, trying to attract my interest. I picked at the omelet in front of me instead. Vivian was astonished. "It's from Bill and Melinda Gates. A condolence note. They want me to come stay with them when I feel up to it. Can you believe it?"

I took the note from her and threw it in a pile on the counter with about a hundred others. Notes, letters, and flowers had been pouring in all day. "Yeah."

"Can't you feel the love? So many people are touched by what happened to us. Your father was so admired."

"You're getting off on playing the role of the tragic widow, aren't you?"

Vivian cringed at my insult. But I knew I was spot on. How on earth was I supposed to co-exist with this woman for the rest of the summer?

The will had been specific. Vivian was to be my guardian until I turned eighteen, when my inheritance kicked in. It was a shitload of money. Vivian got a bunch too. Then, apparently, there were several charities and other smaller beneficiaries. Vivian had explained it all to me but I hadn't listened.

There was more blah blah blah from Viv about how our housekeeper took the time to make my favorite meal, and I needed to eat something. I needed to get out. I needed to get on with life.

I tuned it all out. It had been three days since the reading of the will, and I had spent most of it in my bedroom. There was a knock at the front door. Ten seconds later, I was surrounded by Viv's gaggle of friends. They were gushing over the letters, "Oohing" and "Ahhing" over the flowers. I had to get out of there.

I didn't know where I was going until I found myself pulling into the driveway of the cemetery. I stopped the car when I saw a woman kneeling at my father's grave. I was puzzled, didn't recognize her from the back. It was weird to walk on top of people, but there was no official pathway to the gravesite. I got pretty close before the woman was even aware of my presence. I startled her. She turned a tearstained face up to me. Such grief on her face. More than I had seen on Vivian's face. Even more than I had seen looking in the mirror.

"Who are you?"

The woman hesitated. Instead of answering, she said, "You're his daughter. You're Cassidy." She spoke with the slightest hint of an accent.

"I know who I am. The question is, who the hell are you?"

"I guess it doesn't matter now. No point in secrecy. The sneaking. The hiding. All done."

I had run out of patience. "What are you talking about? Why are you here? Why are you crying?"

"My name is Clara. I loved your father. And he loved me."

I narrowed down the accent to somewhere in Eastern Europe. "Why should I believe you?"

"I don't care if you do or not. It's the truth. We were lovers for nine months."

I had no idea…I mean, I'm sure Vivian didn't either. I know he and my stepmom had problems, and, of course, my dad was not above a little adultery every once in a while, but I was skeptical Dad had fallen deeply in love. There was nothing tying him to Vivian. If he wanted to, he could have kicked her out any time.

Clara got specific. "At first it was just a fling. Nothing serious. I didn't want to settle down. I'm a journalist. I love to travel. We would meet up in different places. Your father was very charming and very good looking, as you know. It was fun. That's all. Just a good time."

This woman's voice got pretty grim, her look intense. She was really working herself up, tears filled her eyes again. I was surprisingly calm. It made sense to me that Dad had a little chicky on the side. I should have just let it go. I should have walked away. But I didn't. Something made me stay and press for answers. I got the feeling Clara felt very alone in her grief. My heart softened towards her.

"I remember the exact moment I fell in love with Hudson. We were laying on the sand in Mexico. It was sunset. This was months ago."

"Yeah, possible. I remember Dad being gone a couple of times recently. On business."

"He hated lying, cheating. We didn't start out wanting anything long-lasting. Our first time, I thought it would just be a one-night stand. We met in a bar in New York. I knew he was married. He told me about his wife and daughter. I didn't ask for details. I liked being with him in a casual way. That first time we parted, I never thought I'd see him again. But he called me. I hadn't given him my phone number. But somehow he managed to get it."

"Yeah. Dad is…I mean was into computer microchips and shit like that. Technology…was his thing. And he had a bunch of geniuses working for him. If he wanted to hack into someone's computer or get information of any kind, he could. Getting your cell number was probably a cinch."

"We saw each other again. In Chicago. Then again in Paris. Each time was more wonderful, more passionate, more amazing than the time before. I'm sorry. It's insensitive of me to talk this way to you."

"It's okay. I'm not blind. I know my dad was a player. No illusions about that. Go on. I want to hear everything. Believe me, I have no loyalty to Vivian."

"When we were in Mexico, a few months ago, I told him I was in love with him. He knew. We had never said the words before but he knew…even before I did. He told me he was in love with me too and that he was only happy when he was with me. You would have thought that would be a perfect moment. But it wasn't. I hadn't signed up for this. It was too much. I got up and told him I needed to be alone for a while. I started walking down the beach. I had to sort out my thoughts. I never set out to break up a family.

"I finally went back to the room. I told him we had a problem. He didn't see it that way. He told me he could handle it. He could handle anything. We talked all night. He told me how sad he was when your mom died. Even though they were divorced at the time, he truly was hurt. I saw him cry over a picture of her. He was a strong man, but he could be tender too. He married Vivian too soon, before he'd gotten his feet back under him. He didn't hate Vivian, but he didn't love her either. He described her as mercenary…as shallow…vain. The more he lived with her the more he felt sucked into her world. I guess you live in a very tight-knit community. Everybody seems to know everyone. Everyone is wealthy and driven and competitive."

"Yeah."

"He wanted out. We made plans. We were going to turn our lives upside down for each other. I was going to quit my job and be with him. We were going to disappear. He was going to sell his company and get a divorce from Vivian. He was so happy…the idea of being free of that lifestyle, that life that was choking him. He was losing his soul."

"What about me?"

"He wanted you to go to college, build a life for yourself, but he never wanted to lose you. He planned on telling you everything, making sure you had anything and everything you needed. He wanted to escape the world but not you. He would have told you where we were. He wanted to be with you as much as possible, and he didn't think you'd have a problem with me or the fact that he was leaving. He said you hated the life Vivian had created for you as much has he did."

"I guess I do. I have friends…close friends. But I didn't…I mean I don't feel trapped. Not the way my dad did. I was always going to leave when I turned eighteen. I knew I could always come back and see him any time I wanted, that he would always be a part of my life. Looking back, I realize now how miserable he was. He kind of took it out on me and my stepmom."

Clara reached out a hand and gently touched my father's freshly-dug grave. She slowly traced her fingers over the temporary headstone. "I can't believe he's gone. I read it in the papers…what happened. I just don't believe it. I can't believe some insane accident took his life."

"I know. Me neither. But it did."

"Did it?"

"Well, yeah. He was drunk, did something stupid."

"Even drunk, your father was never stupid. Maybe his judgment was impaired, but I can't believe his death was just a case of bad timing."

"What are you saying?"

"Maybe it's the journalist in me, but I can't leave it alone. This man was the love of my life and now he's dead? I can't accept that. I told him that his wife would never let him go. I never met Vivian but I'd heard a lot about her from your father. Let me ask you something, where were you when your father died?"

"I was right there."

"And where was your stepmother?"

"She was there in the garage with him, arguing. He got in the car to get away from her. We both saw the whole thing."

"They must have been arguing about me. She would have been furious at the idea of being left…divorced. It wouldn't have mattered how much your father was willing to pay her. I know her kind. She wouldn't have let him go."

"What are you saying?"

"I think your stepmother had a hand in your father's death."

"Murdered? Don't most people use a gun or a knife or poison or something a little more specific. Death by garage door? Never heard of it. Besides I saw it. I gave my statement to the police. It was pretty cut and dried even if it was a bloody, gory nightmare."

Clara wouldn't give up. "But he died just as he's leaving her? I don't believe in coincidences. And she was there."

I felt my knees buckling under me. I sank to the ground. I was "processing" again. Clara pulled out her cell phone, pulled up a photo, and showed it to me. It was a picture of her with my dad, arms around each other, looking very much in love.

"Okay. So you and Dad were in love. I can buy that. But Vivian killing him? I don't think so."

"But you're not sure now, are you? I see doubt in your eyes. I quit my job so I could be with him forever. And now I have no job, no hope, no chance at ever loving again. All that is left to me is despair. Maybe I'm just crazy with grief. But I keep asking myself over and over, could a man that wonderful, that magnificent die that way? My money's on Viv."

And then I remembered, "She did say the oddest thing after the funeral. I accused her of egging my dad on, that maybe if she hadn't been screaming at him at the top of her lungs, this all might not have happened. And she totally copped to it."

Clara's clear blue-grey eyes widened. We sat there quietly, and then Clara said, "I knew it. Vivian killed your father."

"It wasn't a confession, it's just a weird thing for her to say. Maybe she feels guilty because they were fighting when he drove out. She saw his head rip off...I mean, Damn...that's gotta fuck up your thinking. Don't read too much into what she said. We don't have any proof she did anything wrong."

"I'll get proof."

"How?"

"I'm an amazing investigative journalist."

Clara smiled, and I could see how Dad could fall in love with her. She was breathtaking. White blonde hair cut straight across the cheek line. Flawless skin and a body I would kill to have. Yeah, Dad would have appreciated all those things in her. But what I appreciated was that, as drop-dead gorgeous as she was, she was just that smart. And I was starting to believe in her…at least in her story about taking Dad away from Vivian forever, especially after the strange conversation I'd had with an unusually insecure Viv that morning. All those questions about why Dad had married her. She truly seemed perplexed. She copped to the fact that Dad didn't love her, never did. So Dad was an easy target for someone as amazing as Clara. Well, whatever reasons Dad had for marrying my stepmother, they had seemed to have gone away in those last days. If Clara was telling the truth, he was ready to throw Viv over in a heartbeat. Only he never got the chance.

❧

When I got back from the cemetery, Vivian was alone. I was surprised, sure that her cadre of buddies would be through their second Bloody Mary by now. But she was alone, on the floor, a cardboard box near her, papers all over the floor, and tears streaming down her face. I didn't care for the woman, but I wasn't a monster either. I rushed to her.

"What's wrong?"

"I inherited a lot more than money today. I got all his private files. I've been skimming through most of them…pretty boring stuff. But then I found this one. Look. It's a note from the board of directors. They all signed it. Look at the date. It was right after old man Tate had died and the CEO job was up for grabs."

I took the letter and read through it quickly. While the board heartily endorsed my father as CEO for his brains and his cunning in making deals and undercutting competitors, they were worried about his reputation. He was known to be a little too wild in his ways. Too many parties, drugs, and women. I skimmed down to the end of the letter which basically gave my father an ultimatum. He needed to mend his ways, become a mature, solid citizen, an upright family man, or the job would go to someone else.

I let the letter fall from my hand as I looked up at Viv's tearstained face. The implications were pretty obvious. He did his research. He found a steady, unattractive, smart woman who gave him an air of legitimacy. My father married my stepmother as a business move. My heart almost broke for Viv. Then again, it had also broken for Clara. Damnit to hell, this was a shitty situation.

Still, there was no excuse for what my dad had done to Vivian, and I didn't pull away when she reached to hug me, desperately looking for comfort. I just couldn't deny her my sympathy. Suddenly, sweet memories of Daddy were starting to be replaced by the reality of who he really was. As Vivian wept, I vowed never to let a man use me. I still believed in true love. And maybe my father truly had it with Clara. But at such a cost.

Viv was mumbling something through her tears. At first I couldn't understand. But then I deciphered the words…"If I'd known this, I would have gladly let the bastard go."

MARGARET

June 2

6

I ROLLED DOWN MY CAR WINDOW and yelled as loudly as I could. It was most undignified.

"Margaret Cranston. I'm here to see my daughter, Lisa Roth. I've been here a million times. Why do you have to check that stupid clipboard? Don't you recognize me?"

I was at the guard's station entrance to the gated community of Avalon Estates. I appreciated the security the guards afforded my daughter and her family, but honestly, did they really have to use such cautionary measures with a seventy-six-year-old woman?

"I'm sorry, Mrs. Cranston, of course I know you. I just have to follow procedure."

I looked at the guard's nametag. They say you get more flies with honey than vinegar. Well, I was too old to give a damn about attracting anything or anyone. Growing old was an annoying process. While I enjoyed excellent health for a woman my age, time and gravity were taking its toll. The upside to being my age is I could be as forthright, or even downright rude if I wanted to, and no one would take umbrage. I took advantage of this often.

"Rudy, you don't look like a stupid man. So please don't act like one. If I catch you checking my license plate or my name one more time, I'll insist my daughter move her family out of this pretentious housing tract immediately. And I'll call your superior and make sure he knows you're to blame. Do you understand?"

"Yes, Ma'am."

I can appear quite formidable when I want to. I had Rudy quaking in his boots. As the gate opened and I headed down the lane towards Lisa's house, I felt a little guilty. It was my acting training, you see. I had enjoyed a brief stint on the stage in the late 70's, and I could play a crotchety old woman very well. But it was all an act. Anyone who really knows me, sees me for the soft-hearted woman that I really am. That doesn't mean I can't be tough when I want. I buried two husbands, both of whom I loved dearly. I'd been forced to declare bankruptcy several times, only to recoup my financial losses with some very tricky day trading success on the market.

Currently, I was quite flush and enjoying an affluent lifestyle. I pulled into Lisa's driveway just as she dashed out of the front door to meet me.

"Mom, what the hell are you driving?"

"I just bought it. It's a Rolls Royce Phantom. I've always wanted one. Don't you like it?"

"You look ridiculous in it."

"I look regal."

"Well, I can't argue that, Mother. Come inside. I'll make you some tea. And then, I have the most amazing story to tell you."

We entered the house. Lisa called it a mansion but it was too new… too lacking in character to be a true mansion. It was one of those overblown, stone and column monstrosities that take up the entire lot.

There were no grounds to speak of. The houses on either side of it were just as large, but the lots themselves were bigger. Oh well, if it was all Carson could afford…who was I to be snobbish. I did enjoy the view from the back patio. The house backed up against the lake, which was lovely any time of day. A few of the houses had electric boats docked against piers which jutted from their backyards to the water. But Lisa and her husband, Carson, hadn't bothered building a pier or buying a boat. The lake was real estate eye candy to them, nothing more. And while the water was pristine and perfectly safe, no one ever swam in it. *What a waste*, I thought.

Lisa brought me a cup of tea, but seeing as it was four o'clock, I insisted on sherry.

The sound of children shouting at each other could be heard from above. I could barely hear Lisa above the din.

"Can't you control those children?"

The tea splashed all over the place as Lisa poured it, "You know I can't."

The front door opened and in walked my son-in-law, Carson. He was not a bad-looking man but not handsome either. He was balding but had kept physically fit. He had piercing blue eyes. If I had one complaint about his appearance, it was that his nose didn't fit his face. I suspected a bad plastic surgery job but couldn't be sure. Whenever I looked at him…well, *that* nose with *that* face…he just reminded me a little of a pig. I know—I'm a terrible person.

He wore a suit custom-made for him by a Savile Row tailor in London, carried a briefcase from Italy, and toted a bundle of Hollywood trade papers under his arms. He kissed Lisa perfunctorily on the lips as she jumped to greet him. It was clear who wore the pants in this family. Carson surveyed the room.

"Lisa, my darling. Oh, hello, Margaret. Are you staying for dinner?"

"No."

"Well, neither am I."

Lisa looked disappointed. "I had Cook make lamb chops and the kids hate them. Why do you have to go out?"

Carson poured himself a drink. "Sandra's going on a press junket tomorrow. I have to prep her. It's her first, you know, quite inexperienced. I wish I could go with her, but I have that fucking James Cameron opening here in town and I can't miss it. Not worth his endless hissy fit if I don't attend. So I gotta go over some stuff with Sandra and the staff before she leaves for China. Huge market over there. We're expecting the film to do very well. But it's tricky. Have to say all the right things, can't be offending anyone. They're very sensitive to Westerners over there."

I couldn't help myself. "Then it's a good thing you're not going, Carson. You're the least sensitive person I know."

Carson was immune to insults. "Aren't you the clever one, Mags. Of all my mother-in-laws, I think you're my favorite. You just tell it like it is. Yes, I never think before I speak so it's probably a damn good thing Sandra's the diplomat for the film."

The noise from upstairs grew louder. It clearly annoyed Carson. "Lisa, can't you do something about those children? A little peace and quiet in this house would be nice."

Lisa was at the end of her rope. "Then you talk to them. They're your kids. They don't respect me."

Carson was determined to prove to her how easy child rearing really is. He hollered, "Kids, get down here. Your father is home."

There was the sound of pounding feet down the stairs, then the three of them stood before us. The antichrists. Wyatt, the fifteen year old, was the first with his complaints, "I finished my homework. I swear I did. So I was playing Halo when these two asswipes come in and start grabbing my controller."

I winced, "Wyatt, must you use that kind of language?"

Wyatt actually liked me and for the most part, we got along. "Sorry, Mags. But you have to agree these two cretins are assholes."

Privately I did agree with Wyatt but wasn't about to say so. Thirteen-year-old Chase and his younger half-brother, nine-year-old Liam, were obnoxious, spoiled, and impossible to manage. They spoke quickly, loudly, and over each other. "It's our turn. We want to play Call of Duty."

Carson didn't see a problem. "Each of you have your own Xbox. Play your own."

Liam reminded him, "I broke mine. Remember I threw it at Dickhead's face."

Lisa barely made an effort, "Don't call Chase that. We've talked about it."

It was Chase's turn to defend himself, "Yeah, well, I retaliated by introducing my tennis racket to not only his Xbox but his Nintendo as well."

Carson laughed, "Oh, I remember now. Lisa, give them some money and I'll have Lupe drive them to pick up new game players. That should solve the problem."

Lisa was just as horrified as I was. "Carson, you can't condone their actions. They destroy each other's things and so you reward them with whatever they want."

Carson was already bored with the situation. He handed Chase and Liam each five hundred dollars. "That ought to do it. Run along now."

The youngest boys took off hooting and hollering. Lupe, the house-keeper, was in for a very unpleasant trip to the mall. Wyatt wordlessly headed up to his room.

I felt very third-wheelish and went off to use the powder room, but stopped around the corner to eavesdrop.

Lisa couldn't help but admonish Carson. "No wonder their mothers don't want them. You've turned them into monsters. And we're stuck with them. And they have no respect for me…none…because you let them treat me like trash."

Carson put down his drink, straightened his tie, and headed for the door. "My children adore me. My first three wives were idiots. I thought I'd done better with you. Obviously not. At least the kids have a hobby. You sit around here doing nothing all day but wait for me to come home. Can't you get a life of your own? You're suffocating the hell out of me. And look at you, you're letting yourself go. Think I want my wife to look like a cow? Why the hell did I hire that personal trainer for you anyway? Your ass is in freefall. And I don't think the chemical peels and Botox are enough. Make an appointment with Ted. He'll do a marvelous job."

Lisa was silent. Then she spoke quietly, trying to hide the wounds her husband's words had inflicted on her. "I'm not getting a facelift or liposuction or anything else. I'm sorry. I work with my trainer every day. I'm a size six for god's sake. I'm hardly huge. I get compliments all the time. Other men think I'm pretty."

"I don't want pretty. I want perfect." And he slammed the door on his way out.

As I rounded the corner, I could barely contain my composure. "How dare you let him talk to you like that?"

Lisa made a drink of her own, "What am I supposed to do, Mother? My prenup is airtight. When I married Carson, I never dreamed in a million years I'd be stuck trying to raise three minions from hell. Or just stand there and take it in the face like that. I swear, Mother, I just don't know how much more of this I can take. I mean it. I love this house. I love my friends. And I hate Carson's job. I thought it would be so cool to be the wife of a big time Hollywood agent. But it sucks. Carson is not the man I married. He's changed. He only cares about his work. There's no space in his heart for me or even for his children. He ignores his boys, abuses me with horrible language, then the minute the phone rings, he turns into Mr. Nice Guy, the savior of the world. Inevitably, the call is from drunken clients at three in the morning needing to be bailed out of jail. Carson's globe-hopping here and there to see some talentless movie star do Hamlet in the West End. He craves the drama of it all. I have begged him over and over, why not represent regular people? There are nice actors out there. But he swears that the nice ones never win Academy Awards, but I know that's not true. Truth is, I think he thrives on the notorious nature of all his clients. They're forever in and out of rehab, or jail, or uttering racial slurs in public. And Carson thinks he's like some kind of god swooping in, doing damage control, and covering their asses. You know what the sad part of it all is? It works. Weeks later, it's all forgotten. The bar fights, the domestic abuse charges. All of it. Carson has a knack for spin. He works the reporters, the judges, everyone. In the blink of an eye, it's all forgotten. But it never stops, Mother, never. I swear, between those miserable children of his and his bullshit job, it's more than a sane person can bear. Oh, it might be different if he truly loved me. But you saw the way he was with me. He meant everything he said. Middle age is creeping up on me, and it won't be long until he throws me out and I'll have nothing."

"I'll take care of you."

"I love you, Mother, but you know we can't live under the same roof without driving each other crazy. Besides, why should I have to give all this up? It's my life. I built it. It means nothing to Carson. But he has all the control. Damn, I hate feeling so powerless!"

I hated seeing my daughter so miserable. I thought back to the day of her wedding. I was married to my second husband at the time. He and I struggled financially. I was happy my daughter was marrying a man of means. She'd lived a very poor life up to that point.

Carson was more than happy to pay for a lavish wedding. At first, I thought it was sweet of him, but it all came at a price. He invited all his sick and twisted friends. They hogged the dance floor with their disgusting gyrations. They did drugs in the bathrooms of the Bel Air Hotel. *The Bel Air, mind you.* One of the youths, a very popular singer named Jason or Jordan or Justin, or something like that, threw up on the ice sculpture. I should have known right then and there. I should have taken Lisa away. But I didn't.

I know myself well. I know myself to be a confident woman. I had married a wonderful man, and for thirty years he treated me with respect and dignity. My second husband was equally doting. We had a happy life, happy but struggling financially. Lisa was not experiencing the same joy. She claimed to love her community and friends, but I had reservations. Yes, I was close to her five best friends. And I liked all of them. Like me, they had all come from middle-class upbringings. They were working women who happened to fall in love with rich men…mostly men who had been married before and carried a lot of baggage from the past and a trunk full of ego.

I couldn't think of one of Lisa's friends who was truly happy in her marriage. Except for maybe Dorothy, but she could hardly count, being the ex-hooker that she was. And I happened to know that her husband was not as well-to-do as the other men. Oh sure, he lived the lush life, but he was a washed-out athlete who was taken care of by his friends.

'"What are you thinking about, Mother?"

"I was just thinking about your friends."

"Oh, I almost forgot. That's why I called you over. Did you hear about Hudson?"

"Of course I did. Nasty business. Such a random and violent way to die. I wanted to go to the funeral but wasn't up for burying a headless man."

Lisa was clearly sickened. "I went. It was open casket. I didn't look, although I heard they put him together quite nicely. Still, he was such an important man. He always filled the room with his power and his presence. I can't imagine Avalon without him."

"And I suppose the family is devastated."

Lisa nodded slowly. "Cassidy is a wreck. She's tried to hurt herself several times. Had to be sedated, poor thing. As for Vivian...well, I can't quite pick up on her mood. She's terribly shaken, naturally. But she seems to be alright. Cards, letters, gifts, and flowers have been streaming into the house."

Something felt off. I told Lisa, "I read the article in *People*. They're making her out to be something of a saint."

Lisa admitted, "It's all rather strange. I mean, her drunken husband drives his head into a garage door, and she's the victim. And she's enjoying the attention. Oh, I shouldn't say that. It's terrible of me to even think it. But I know Viv so well. And Hudson...well, let's face it, he was a dick to her. They were very tense with each other that night...the night of the accident. Vivian had complained that Hudson traveled too much. I knew things weren't going well, but I thought she loved him."

"But now you're not sure."

"I don't know. She's very guarded. She's very quiet. She seems to be focusing on responding to the outpouring of love. And she's trying to take very good care of Cassidy. But there's something different. You would think she would be depressed, despondent. But there's actually a light in her eyes…a bit of a spring to her step."

I was flummoxed. "Seriously?"

Lisa squirmed a bit. "I know. It's impossible to believe and yet true. I was there when the will was read. Hudson was a very generous man, left quite a bit to charity…some to Tommy, of course, and to people I didn't recognize. Yet the bulk of the estate is to be split between Cassidy and Vivian. Even with his assets halved, that still makes Viv a very rich woman. And I keep thinking…. No…I can't say it."

I was on the edge of my seat, "Say it. You can confide in me."

"I've just been envious of Vivian since the funeral. So many people adore her, want to help her, take care of her. And all that money…it's all hers to spend as she pleases. Good God, when Hudson was alive, she had to beg him for everything. No one knew why they were ever together in the first place. She was hardly his type. And this is cruel to say but she's hardly anyone's type. She's my friend and I adore her, but their marriage always seemed cold to me. But hell, who am I to talk. It's just that she's got all the perks of her life with Hudson and none of the downside. And I…well, frankly I envy her."

"You mean you wish Carson were dead."

From upstairs we could hear the sound of shattering glass. I could only assume Wyatt had thrown something out of his bedroom window. "Fuck this game! Fuck my life!"

Lisa looked me dead in the eye and in a clear and sure voice spoke without hesitation said, "It wouldn't be the worst thing in the world."

I was trying to get a good read on Lisa, see if she really meant what she said. Wanting your husband dead was rather drastic.

"Stop staring at me, Mother. I'm just talking…you know, venting."

Lisa ditched her tea and joined me in some sherry as her eyes glanced around the room.

There were almost tears in Lisa's eyes, "Look at this house. There isn't a painting on the wall or a stick of furniture I didn't pick out myself. You know how I love French Provincial. It's my dream house. Carson never cared. I made this house beautiful. And he spends maybe five minutes in it a day…if I'm lucky. And his children…don't get me started. They have no sense of boundaries or decorum. They have no manners or care or concern for anyone but themselves. Egotistical pigs! Their own mothers have pawned them off on us because they're impossible to manage."

"But if Carson were dead, you wouldn't have to deal with the brats, would you?"

Lisa scolded, "Mother, don't say that. I told you, I didn't mean it. I am just on my last nerve, that's all." She checked her watch. "Now, if you'll excuse me. I have to do something with my hair and makeup. The kids can eat Cook's food. I'm having dinner with the girls tonight."

"I was thinking I might take you out to dinner. But if you'd rather…"

"Come with me. We'll go to the club. Very simple. Vivian adores you, and it will be good for her spirits to see you."

"All right. I actually like that strange little group of women. What is their nickname? You know, what everyone calls you behind your back when they don't think you're listening?"

"The Ladies of the Lake. And, Mother, I don't mind it at all." Her voice was unusually edgy with me. I watched as my daughter stared out her back window. The sun was going down, its light reflecting all pink and gold on the water.

Yes, I thought, "The Ladies of the Lake." It was a perfect title for Lisa…for all of them.

We could hear another voice coming from above. It was Wyatt again. "Why can't I get this freakin' thing to go louder. Shit!" Then he put on some obnoxious rap music. I couldn't make out the lyrics except the chorus, which had something to do with various sexual positions.

Lisa looked apologetic. "Just give me five minutes to change." She shot another annoyed look up towards Wyatt's room. "If you can stand it."

？

We arrived last. The round table comfortably seated seven. Lisa took her place and grabbed immediately for the open wine bottle in the middle of the table. I was a little more polite and calm. I greeted each of them, Dotty, Morgan, Anjelica, Crystal, and last but most importantly,

Vivian, who was surprised by our entrance. No one expected us tonight. I explained that Carson, as usual, had bailed. I needed my cane to make my way around the table, but I was determined to hug Vivian. "I'm so terribly sorry for your loss, my dear."

"Thank you, Margaret. Everyone's been so kind. These last few days have been like a dream. I don't mean that in a good way…or a bad way. It's just that I keep expecting Hudson to walk through the door or call or…I don't know what…just be alive. But he's not. And my dear friends from all over the world seem to feel my pain. It's been such an outpouring of love."

We ordered dinner and tried to make small talk, but there was clearly only one topic on everyone's mind. As the dessert cart was shooed away, I decided to broach the subject once more.

"Dear Vivian, I understand what you're going through completely. I mean, the way your husband died is a little more graphic than the way my husbands died—both had garden variety heart attacks. Still, I've felt the pain of widowhood. You never recover."

Even as I was saying this, I was carefully studying Vivian's face, thinking Lisa was right. Vivian looked more than "recovered," she looked as if she'd been paroled.

Vivian said she didn't want to spoil the night with talk on that topic. Couldn't they just forget about the tragedy for an evening and focus on something superficial and shallow? Why don't you all come with me to our house in the Hamptons? We can go to parties and polo matches.

The other women looked wistful at the suggestion. They wanted to, of course. But none of them could. They had family obligations. Vivian was the only free one. Even Crystal had to bow out. It was one of the few weeks Jonathan was actually going to be around. And she would be ovulating…

I stopped her right there. In my day, a woman would never discuss such things in public. Not that we had any idea when we were ovulating. Now all you have to do is go to the drugstore and buy a kit to find out exactly what your ovaries were up to.

Vivian was disappointed. "Well, maybe I'll go anyway. I need a change of pace. The press is finally tired of the story and the police are done with their investigation…so…"

I looked carefully from one woman to the other. There was half-hidden jealousy in every one of their eyes…even Dorothy, who had never shown an interest in attending such events.

Morgan ventured, "Maybe I could get away for a few days. Sheraton is going to be in Bermuda. We could take the girls with us. Maddie and Crystal would have a great time." She checked the calendar on her phone, "Oh no…I'm chairing a luncheon that week…Arts in Education. I'm sorry, Vivian. I know how desperately you've suffered."

I couldn't keep my mouth shut, "You should go, Vivian. You're free to do as you please now. In some ways, you're the most enviable woman at this table. Lisa was just saying earlier…"

I was cut off, "That's enough, Mother." It was time for the evening to end. But none of the women wanted to part company.

"Let's go to my place for drinks," suggested Crystal. "Jonathan won't be home until tomorrow."

"Excellent idea," I chimed in. Then, really taking advantage of the social graces I'm allotted because of my age, I ventured a most shocking suggestion, "May I invite myself along? Because we'll have so much more privacy there. And I think it's time we really opened up to each other about our lives. I've seen lots of happy women in my day, and not one of you looks anything close to happy. And if you're all so damn miserable, we ought to do something about it."

7

CRYSTAL POURED THE WINE. ALL THE Ladies drank hastily. All but me. As I said before, there's an upside to being old and there's a downside. The downside is that I can't enjoy drinking…not the way I used to. Ah well. I wanted to keep my wits about me anyway. Lisa's friends were hell-bent on getting drunk. They made a good start of it at the club, and now that they were safe in the privacy of Crystal's home, the wine flowed freely and tongues loosened. Dotty hadn't been able to join us. So our group was even smaller than usual. Lisa shot me a nasty look. She wasn't thrilled I'd invited myself to the impromptu party. She was afraid I'd say something "insensitive." I usually do. It's my way. My heart broke to see these women live under the yoke of the slavery of their marriages. Their husbands were all bastards. But maybe that topic was off limits.

Lisa was very sensitive to Vivian's feelings. "Don't listen to my mother. She didn't mean what she said. Of course, we all look miserable. Hudson's death has weighed heavily on our hearts."

"Yes, that's right. I'm a doddering old fool. No one here wants to make light of your tragedy, Vivian. I guess I don't take death quite as seriously as the rest of you. Maybe because it's certainly right around the corner for me. At my age, I go to bed every night wondering if I'll wake up in the morning. I don't really worry, I just wonder. Not a bad way to go…in my sleep, my best years behind me."

"What a selfish way to talk," chided my daughter. "Hudson was struck down in the prime of his life. And the subject of death is certainly more complicated than you make it out to be. It's not just the person who dies, it's those they leave behind. Hudson's friends and family are horribly bereft."

I studied Vivian's guarded expression closely before saying. "Yes, I'm sure that's true. I apologize. I seem to be losing my internal filter. I just say what I think these days. No matter how rude or insensitive, out it pops."

Vivian shook her head, "You're an inspiration, Margaret. You're honest. I'd like to be honest. I need to be. I can't sleep at night—not for more than a few minutes at a time. And when I do sleep I have horrible nightmares…the accident."

"Of course you do," said Lisa. "That's to be expected."

Morgan suggested a therapist.

"I'm seeing one. But the nightmares persist. And that's because I feel guilty. There. I said it. I feel responsible for Hudson's death."

A hush fell over the room. No one knew what to say. Finally, Anjelica cleared her throat, "That's silly, honey. The way that man died. It was foolish, to be sure. But it was no one's fault but himself. He closed that door right on his head. Just crazy."

"No. I closed the door. I was just trying to keep him from leaving. I didn't know what would happen. But I did it. I didn't mean to kill him but I did. If I hadn't been so insistent that he stay, he'd be alive today."

Anjelica hugged her, "You're talking nonsense."

"No. What you all don't know is that he was leaving me for another woman. I just couldn't let that happen. I closed the door. I murdered my husband. And I have all these feelings, and I don't know what to do with them. I hate myself. Then I find myself surrounded by caring and concerned people, and that means so much to me that I feel almost happy. Then I feel guilty for feeling happy, and yet I have all this freedom and it does feel…good somehow. I don't know. I'm a horrible person."

All the girls had their arms around Vivian by this point. No one said anything.

Finally, Vivian pulled away and went to pour herself another stiff drink. I felt responsible for Vivian's confession…one she might now be regretting so I took it upon myself to try to soften the situation.

"Look, none of us know what exactly happened. But your husband had betrayed you. You were just trying to salvage your family. That's all. And that's all that ever needs to be said about that. We're never going to judge you or blame you. And you'd be wrong to blame yourself."

Lisa wanted to help too. And, being very drunk, she thought the best way was to commiserate with Vivian.

"I'm pretty sure my husband's going to leave me sometime soon. I feel sick about it…like I'm going to throw up all the time."

The other women gasped at Lisa's bold statement.

Morgan refused to believe it. "Why would he leave you? You're perfect. You take care of his bratty kids when no one else does. You put up with all his work shit. He needs you. There is no good reason for him to leave you."

"Because I'm growing too old for him."

Anjelica scared the hell out of everyone when she threw her wine glass into the wall. "Damn him. I've seen it time and time again. We get traded in for a younger model. We give them everything and we are cast aside. It's disgusting."

Crystal started to pick up the broken pieces. "I'd like to say you're wrong. But that's probably his plan. We all know Carson pretty well, and that sounds like something he would do. That's what Jonathan did with me. I'm the same age as his daughter. I'm nothing but a trophy wife…that and I'm supposed to give him a son…an heir. And we all know how well that's going. He's like fucking Henry VIII. If I don't come up with a baby boy soon, I'll get tossed away. And, as strange as that may seem, to know that about him, about what he's capable of doing to me, I still love him. I think I'm the one who needs a therapist."

Anjelica helped Crystal clean up. "I think we all need to face facts. We made terrible mistakes in choosing the men we married."

Vivian was worried. "You sound angry, Anjelica."

"Not angry. But honest. I know I shouldn't be saying this. Shit, I've had so much to drink, tomorrow I probably won't even remember I have said it. But I have to put my husband in the same category as Lisa's. He's a son-of-a-bitch. I know his job takes him away a lot. I'm glad he gets as many movie roles as he does. But I don't trust him. I don't know what he does when he's on those sets. He never invites me to join him."

"Jonathan's gone a lot, too…on business," Crystal mumbled into her glass. She looked like she was about to keel over.

Morgan was the only one who seemed to be able to hold her wine, "My husband's gone a lot, too. That's part of the deal. You marry a rich, successful man, he's got a lot of responsibilities. That doesn't mean he's not to be trusted."

Once Anjelica started to unload her fears and worries, she couldn't seem to stop. "You may believe that load of crap, Morgan, but I don't. I think men are incapable of being monogamous. I'm willing to admit the truth about Alphonse. He's having an affair, I just know it. Ha. Probably more than one. He's clever. He keeps it all from the press. But when he comes home from a shoot…I can just tell. He brings me presents and makes a fuss over me, but he doesn't do these things because he loves me. He does them out of guilt. Secrecy and guilt. I'm sick of both of them. Margaret, you were right when you said we were all miserable. We live lives of luxury and yet we're all unhappy in our marriages."

Crystal couldn't hear anymore, and she seemed to just blackout. She fell over slowly, her face planting on the "death by chocolate cake" they were all sharing. As if in slow motion, she moaned…. "Secrecy… guilt…Jonathan…"

Vivian saw it first. "Oh dear. We'd better take her upstairs and put her to bed."

Morgan shook her head, "I'm too drunk to carry anybody. And I'm sure as hell too drunk to drive. I'm walking home."

Anjelica put down her glass and stumbled towards the front door. "I'm afraid I'm in the same condition. I'm going home too. I'll check on Crystal in the morning. Good night."

Vivian looked down at Crystal, "I guess I could try to get her upstairs."

Lisa was practical. "Viv, none of us would be strong enough to lift her if we were sober. Face it, Morgan. We have to leave her. Let's just get her face out of the cake, put a blanket over her, and let her sleep down here."

Morgan wiped Crystal's face and tucked her in, "I just hope Jonathan doesn't come home and find her like this. He's not a very understanding person."

8

FOUR DAYS LATER, IT BECAME ABUNDANTLY apparent that Jonathan was not an understanding person. I was having breakfast with Lisa at my favorite restaurant in Malibu, near my home. As I said before, I was doing very well financially, and I enjoyed living near the beach. I even occasionally took a swim in the ocean, something that shocked my daughter.

"Mother, I don't even use the pool at the club. None of my friends do. It's unsettling the way you throw yourself into the surf. At your age, you'll probably drown. You need to be careful."

"Why?" I took a sip of my mimosa and relished the taste. "I don't have many years left. I might as well have a good time. Besides, the doctor said swimming is good for me."

"He expected you to take a water aerobics class for the elderly at the beach club or something. I can just imagine now, calling the Coast Guard, having them search for your body."

"Don't worry about me. I'm not ready to go just yet."

As the waiter brought our food, I noticed a familiar face entering the restaurant. It was Crystal. I pointed her out to Lisa, and we called her over to our table. She was wearing a running suit and state-of-the-art running shoes. She was out of breath and more than a little sweaty. She didn't look pleased to see us but she agreed to sit down for a moment and chat.

"I was just jogging on the boardwalk. It's so beautiful down here, it's worth the drive."

Lisa was a bit surprised. "I thought you were more of a gym rat."

"I do free weights, too. Today I just felt like getting out."

She ordered a protein smoothie and took off her sweatshirt. What we saw alarmed Lisa. "What are those marks on your arm?"

I knew immediately, of course. There were five small bruises on her forearm. Basically the size of fingertips. Someone had grabbed her rather tightly. Crystal quickly covered up.

"Oh, nothing. You know me. I'm such a klutz. As a matter of fact, I don't even remember doing it. Maybe it happened after you left the other night. I'm still so embarrassed that I passed out like that. I'm such a lightweight. I wish I could hold my liquor the way the rest of the girls do. I'm going to have to start slowing down."

I didn't want to point out the obvious, but Lisa was too concerned to be polite. "Those bruises aren't from a fall. Someone grabbed you. It was Jonathan, wasn't it?"

Crystal's face turned to stone. She got up just as her drink was being served. She threw a ten down on the table and tore into Lisa. "You know, some things are private. We are friends, but there's such a thing as boundaries. I think we crossed a lot of them the other night. I don't know what I said in my drunken stupor…"

Lisa tried to diffuse, "Not that much. We were all kind of in a husband-bashing mood. Especially off that shocking confession Vivian made." She turned to me. "My mother is quite the instigator. She got us all complaining about our lives, which is ridiculous since we are so blessed and so financially comfortable. Anjelica is the one who went off about Alphonse. I'm really quite worried about her. She's sure he's cheating on her, which I guess is part of the deal when you marry an actor with a wandering eye. Crystal, you really didn't say much. And I'm sorry if I insinuated anything was amiss between you and Jonathan. It's really none of my business. Please don't go. Your smoothie just got here. Relax. We'll talk about something else."

But there was no appeasing Crystal. "I have to go anyway. I'll see you later."

Before we could say another word of protest, she was gone. Lisa gave me a dirty look. I felt compelled to defend myself.

"What are you looking at me for? I didn't say anything. I didn't have to. I've seen physically abused women before. God help them, they never seem to want to admit the truth. Maybe I was the instigator the other night, but I know enough to keep my mouth shut when I see something like that. You can't get her to say a bad word about Jonathan when she's sober. She worships him. Battered women. It's a syndrome."

"Well, I've never seen a mark on her before. And you heard her before she passed out. If she hadn't been so drunk, I think she would have opened up more about her marriage. It seemed like she was on the verge of agreeing with Anjelica about men and how they can't keep their marriage vows. She obviously thinks Jonathan's cheating on her. He's always off on one of his damn trips. And he's got no reason to go. His real estate business runs itself. Poor Crystal. She worships Jonathan. And she so badly wants to give him a baby."

"A baby. At his age. That's nonsense. And he's got a perfectly wonderful granddaughter he doesn't give a damn about. Misogynist pig."

"Yes. His daughter, Jessica, is from his first marriage, which ended about a million years ago. Jessica married some guy named Charles who doesn't do anything at all but sit on his ass and live off his father-in-law. They live in upstate New York. They have a daughter named Alison. But Jonathan wants to hand his empire over to a son. And Crystal hasn't been able to get pregnant. She doesn't really like to talk about it and, of course, it's very personal. But we have tried to be supportive of her.

We've even done some research, helped her find the best doctors and treatment available."

"By 'we' I suppose you mean you and the other 'Ladies'."

"Yes, of course. But this whole idea is primeval. Why does he need a male heir? Not that I'm any big fan of Jessica. I've met her a few times, and she is so vapid it's intolerable. And she's not happy that her dad wants to hand everything over to a child who hasn't even been born yet. It's all very twisted. I'm not against Crystal having a baby. Of course she wants a child of her own. But her desperate need to have one stems from her unbalanced desire to please Jonathan, and it just turns my stomach."

I couldn't help myself, "I know I'm going to make you mad, but I simply have to point out that you are hardly one to judge the health of someone else's marriage. You let Carson walk all over you. You take care of his little sons-of-bitches even though they don't have one iota of respect for you. Carson isn't around much more than Jonathan. You need to take a good look in the mirror, darling."

"It's statements like that which make me realize I could never live with you. Of course Carson and I are on the brink of disaster. You don't need to twist the knife."

"Well, then stay with your revolting husband. I'm going to enjoy my last years in peace. Now, if you'll excuse me, I'm going for a swim. If I don't come back, don't bother sending the Coast Guard. I wouldn't want to put you to the trouble."

I knew it was childish of me to end the conversation that way but I didn't care. Lisa was in a terribly dysfunctional marriage, and until she was willing to admit it, there really wasn't much more for us to say.

9

IMAGINE MY SURPRISE WHEN I PICKED up my phone the next day and Crystal was on the other end, her voice ringing with excitement. She was speaking so fast, I couldn't interject a word. She was talking ninety miles an hour.

"I'm so sorry I was edgy the other day, Margaret. I know you didn't mean to insult me or my husband. I was just in a very testy mood. I have news, which will assure you that Jonathan and I are doing better than ever. He's been home for a week now with no plans to go out of town in the immediate future. He's out playing golf with his buddies right now. And he's absolutely ecstatic. Know why? I'm pregnant!"

I paused for a moment. I knew Jonathan had been unkind and perhaps physically rough with Crystal, and I didn't see how adding a baby to the mix was going to help anything. But for once, I kept my opinion to myself.

"Margaret? Are you there?"

"Yes, just letting the glory of the news sink in."

"I've called all the other gals, but I wanted to let you know personally. I'm sorry we had tension between us and I wanted to…"

I stopped her right there. "You've apologized already, and you shouldn't have at all. I've had my share of bad days. You didn't offend me at all. And I couldn't be happier for you."

Crystal was Lisa's friend. Not mine. My big mouth had caused enough damage. I wanted to stay out of this mess. But apparently that wasn't going to happen.

"Margaret, I would just love it if you would join us all for dinner tonight at the club. Jonathan wants to celebrate."

When you're seventy-six years old, one can use a myriad of excuses to beg out of a social engagement. But the rascal in me nudged me to attend. I wanted to see Jonathan, look him in the eyes. I hadn't seen him in a very long time, and I knew just an hour or so in his presence would confirm my bad opinion of him.

"Crystal dear, I would be delighted."

"That's wonderful. See you at seven."

10

THE TIGHT-KNIT CLAN OF FRIENDS WERE all assembled when I arrived. Even their children were in attendance. Lisa had obviously kept an eye out for me because she waved to me from the middle of the clubhouse dining room. The gang had co-opted two large tables in the middle of the room: the traditional "grown-ups" table and one for the kids. Although you could hardly call most of them kids. I knew some of them were about to head off to college soon.

I went over to say my hellos. The men had obviously gotten a head start on the Ladies when it came to liquor. They still had their golfing attire on, so I could only assume they'd drank their way through eighteen holes.

Everyone was extremely polite and fussed over me, labeling me the official matriarch of the group, though I rarely saw them all together.

I worked very hard not to flinch when Alphonse wrapped his arms around me and kissed first one cheek then the other. I've never been fond of exuberance but I went with it. I looked over his shoulder at his wife, Anjelica. She smiled and shrugged. Alphonse was an actor. He had to make a scene everywhere he went.

Fortunately, I was greeted by Sheraton and Morgan with a little more restraint. He seemed to have been the only man who hadn't played golf, as he was wearing an incredibly expensive suit.

I couldn't help but comment, "Sheraton, you look so handsome. Didn't you join the boys on the course today?"

"Yes, actually I did, but I took the time to shower and change. Morgan dressed me. She has excellent taste, don't you think?"

Morgan shook her head as if to deny having anything to do with her husband's appearance.

"You're the handsomest man in the room. If you were thirty years younger, I'd snatch you up for myself."

Lisa was embarrassed. "Mother, stop flirting and sit down."

"Not yet, I haven't said all my hellos."

Tommy and Dotty greeted me with a friendly wave, but didn't get up as they were busy wolfing down appetizers.

Then I made my way over to Jonathan and Crystal. Jonathan offered me his hand, which was soft and manicured. I stifled a wince. I never could abide lazy men, and this one had never worked a day in his life. I gave Crystal a brief kiss on the cheek and congratulated them both on their wonderful news. (I can be a wonderful hypocrite when necessary.)

Cassidy ran up to me and hugged me as tightly as if I were her own grandmother. "Mags, I haven't seen you in so long. I'm so glad you're here."

"Darling, what a young lady you are now. Hardly that little tomboy who ran around the grounds climbing trees and doing belly flops in the pool."

"Oh Mags, that was like a decade ago."

"I'm so sorry about your father."

Tears started to fill her eyes, but she held them back. I admired her restraint.

"Thank you. I think I'm still in shock. I guess it will sink in eventually. It's not that he's gone, it's the way he went. So random. I have been in therapy and my doctor keeps talking about closure. That's a long way off."

She shot a strange look over to her stepmother. I wondered what was going on there. Before I could digest this undercurrent of tension, Cassidy was pulling me over to her friends. Note: Never pull or tug at a seventy-six-year-old woman. It's a recipe for a fall. But Cassidy was so happy to see me, I let the indiscretion go and heavily relied on my cane. I said my hellos to Tommy and Dorothy's adopted son, Zac, Sheraton and Morgan's daughter, Madelyn, and Alphonse and Angelica's daughter, Alana. I also met James, who was Sheraton's son from his first marriage. I immediately liked James. He didn't have his father's obvious stick up his ass. In fact, as a whole, I was keen on all the youngsters. It's as if they'd watched their parents make endless bad decisions, habitually stroke their own egos, and engage in hurtful and destructive gossip and decided to go another way with their lives. These kids were going through a rough patch, to be sure. But I observed the way they smiled at each other, gave each other loving hugs, playful shoves, and warm smiles. They were obviously fiercely loyal to each other.

By the time I made my way to my place with the rest of the adults, the toasts had begun. The men lifted their glasses and drank to the health of the new child they were sure was going to be a boy. Jonathan teared up a little. (He acted like a…I think the word the younger generation uses is *wuss*.) He wished his father could be here. He was determined to name the baby after his dad—the one who made all the money. His father's name had been Fred or Ned, I couldn't make it out between the sniffles.

Crystal looked mortified. She tugged on Jonathan's coat. He seemed very annoyed at the interruption. Crystal tilted her head towards Vivian. Jonathan was three sheets to the wind and beyond understanding the subtle hint. Crystal steeled herself and did the unimaginable. She took Jonathan to task in public.

"Jonathan, I think there's someone else missing. Someone we miss dearly and who left us so recently."

Jonathan's face turned red, not out of embarrassment but out of anger, which he barely kept in check.

"I *know* that, Darling. He was my friend more than yours. We boys missed him terribly on the course today. I almost felt as if we should have set a place for him. I was going to get around to toasting to his memory, but you seem to have stolen my thunder."

Crystal almost shrank into her seat. "I'm sorry. This celebration just doesn't feel complete without Hudson here."

I looked over to Cassidy who had her head down. Zac had his arm around her. Then I looked over at Vivian. She seemed more concerned with diffusing the situation than her own grief.

"Please, Crystal, Jonathan, don't worry about it. Hudson wouldn't want to damper this moment. Let's carry on. I'm sure he's smiling at us from above."

The women immediately leaned into Crystal and started chatting about the practical things women discuss when a baby is on the way. How did she find out? When was she due? Did she feel any nausea? Has she picked the designer for the nursery?

The effect of this onslaught of chatter was a clear signal to Jonathan to sit down, that the toasts were over. It was obvious to everyone that he was very displeased but not wanting to cause a scene, he took his seat. His buddies, wanting to soothe him, continued with pats on the back and the makings of a plan to enjoy cigars on the patio later to fully complete the celebration.

I leaned in to hear Crystal's early pregnancy report. She explained that she recently had an outpatient procedure to correct a problem with one of her fallopian tubes. Oh dear, more medical talk. I simply found it impossible to comprehend how such private matters were proper topics for dinner conversation. No one else seemed to have a problem with it, and the gals expressed dismay that she had gone through such a traumatic experience without their aid. Crystal assured them it wasn't traumatic at all and it only took an afternoon. Vivian asked if Jonathan went with her. Crystal put on a bright smile and said, "No, Jonathan doesn't care for doctor's offices or hospitals." She was quick to make it clear that Jonathan would be at her side for the birth. She looked over at him. There was such a look of adoration. I couldn't imagine why.

Crystal told the Ladies that the doctor thought she was only about seven weeks along, but she was delighted to find out so soon. There was so much to do. She had a nursery to design, a nanny to hire, pregnancy yoga classes to take. She'd already completely changed her diet and was on a strict vitamin regimen.

The other women, most of whom had been through this thing before, were full of advice. I had given birth only once. Lisa was my only child. Even then, I hadn't felt the "glow" of pregnancy nor understood the "miracle" of birth. Women had been having babies every day, all over the world since the beginning of time. The subject bored me.

After I finished my main course, I told Lisa I was too full to handle dessert and decided to take a stroll outside.

11

SHOULD A WOMAN MY AGE SMOKE? Of course not. But I indulged every once in a while, more and more all the time. What could it hurt? I wasn't worried about my lungs or my health in general. I enjoy smoking and plan to do the things I enjoy. But Lisa came unglued every time she caught me, so I was trying to be discreet and find a secluded corner outside to take a few puffs before I bade goodnight to Lisa and her friends. I had watched them deal with news after a death and a new life in the same night. The men, whom I knew were very good friends of Hudson, didn't seem to be particularly upset about the loss of their buddy. I knew the women had a real love for Vivian and a concern for her loss and her feelings of guilt. None of Viv's friends were going to hold her accountable for what had happened. In fact, I think they were very interested in how things were going to turn out for the recently widowed lady.

I thought I had found complete privacy when I heard a hushed, female voice around the corner of one of the cabanas next to the club's pool. I paused. It was not my initial intention to spy, but before I could move away I heard a sentence that froze me in my tracks.

"Don't know. I'm trying to get the paperwork from the garage door repair company. I know it's a long shot. I mean it's an impossible set of circumstances. Vivian would have had to have purposefully provoked Dad into the garage, *assumed* he would choose to drive the convertible, and made sure that he would be drunk, not paying attention, and pushed the button at exactly the right time, freezing the door half open. I think there's no way this could be anything but a stupid accident, and for us to try to prove otherwise and get the police involved is just going to make us look stupid."

I shrunk back into the shadows. I recognized the voice. It was Cassidy, Hudson's daughter. I dropped the cigarette, twisted the red sole of my Louboutin on it, and held my breath. I could hardly believe what I was hearing. She had misgivings about her father's death? She suspected Vivian in playing an active part in the death? And who was she talking to? I peered around the corner. She was on a cell phone. She listened for a moment then responded.

"Well, the police did test the garage opener and they didn't find anything wrong. It didn't seem to perform in any strange way. They pushed the button, it opened. But they don't know that Vivian had her hand on the button. And even if they did know, it doesn't prove anything."

So, Cassidy knew Vivian had pushed the button. This could be trouble. Whom on earth could she be talking to?

"No, Vivian doesn't seem to be as wigged out. She's not crying, she's not depressed. She's spending her time shopping and going to lunch. Maybe she's not so sad Dad's dead. That doesn't make her a murderer. And I was so drunk, maybe I saw it all wrong. I'd hardly be a reliable witness."

Another pause. And then, "I'm not going to get between you two. You were my dad's mistress. And Dad was a bastard to marry Viv just to become the top dog. If you want to go after Vivian because you think of her as some kind of enemy, that's your business."

Before she could say anymore, I saw a shadowy figure approach Cassidy. It was Zac.

"Cass, you okay? Who are you talking to?"

Cassidy hung up without saying goodbye. She clearly didn't want Zac to know anything. "Oh some girl in my debutante group. We're supposed to put this fashion show together before the end of summer but, of course, I don't want to bother. All I can think about is my dad."

Zac put a friendly arm around her. "Dinner seems over. Can we get out of here? James wants us all to go over to his place. We can unwind, forget about all this stuff. It's not that I'm not happy for Jonathan and Crystal, but it's bullshit that they're partying their asses off before your dad's even cold."

"Yeah. I'm not much into babies anyway."

"Then let me take care of you. Let's go, okay?"

I saw Cassidy hug Zac. I know a lot about men and women. These two teenagers were not romantic with each other yet, but things were clearly heading that way.

The two kids left, and I found Lisa and told her I was going home. I was happy for Crystal, gave her a goodbye hug, and told her I'd had a lovely time. But secretly, I had found the last half of the evening far more interesting than the party itself.

CLARA

June 16

12

I REALIZED THE TRIP WAS A mistake the moment I stepped off the plane. The humid, Mexican heat hit me so hard I struggled to breathe. By the time I took a seat inside a taxi, I had shed a scarf and a sweater. I'd boarded the plane in Denver where I'd been covering a story about a massive forest fire. I was a ball of sweat after deplaning onto the Zihuatanejo airport tarmac. How insane was I to make this trip? I had just gotten my life back together, just gotten back into the swing of things at work…and what do I do? I take a week off to come back to the place where I first realized I was in love with Hudson. Why was I torturing myself? Did my subconscious drive me here seeking closure? Or was I so obsessed that I had to cling to each memory, drive it deep into my heart so that it would never fade and I would never let go?

But that's insanity. I had to free myself from Hudson. He was dead.

I kicked myself for luring his daughter into some sort of bogus investigation, some vain attempt to prove that his death hadn't been the result of a random set of circumstances.

I looked out the taxi's window at the rundown buildings and dirty streets of the outskirts of the city. I was a reporter by training and by nature. When something happened, either terrible or wonderful, I had to know the cause. And my hunches and instincts had served me well in the past. My specialty was re-opening closed cases. I'd haunted dozens of police stations all over the country looking for answers to questions they had stopped asking years ago. To me, there was no such thing as an unsolvable crime. I just didn't know if a crime had been committed. I had a hunch and that was all I was going on now.

I found out about Hudson's death the way the rest of the world found out, on television. I had been packing. We were going away together forever. Before Hudson, I never thought I would ever want to meld my life to someone else's. Marriage was a joke. No one stayed together anymore. I was a strong, independent woman, and I fully intended on staying that way. Even after that first encounter with Hudson. I liked him. I was clearly drawn to him sexually. But that was all. At first.

How was I supposed to mourn the love of my life? I felt as if I'd been split in half. Part of me hated that I had ever met Hudson. That was my brain talking. Had I never met Hudson, my heart wouldn't ache so much I could hardly breathe. It would beat. But without Hudson, it had just become an organ keeping my body alive.

I couldn't very well go to the funeral. I couldn't say my final goodbye. I couldn't let go. Maybe that's why I wasn't satisfied with the story of his gruesome and accidental death. Over the years, I had developed a pretty healthy instinct, and something inside me was tugging, nagging…it was no accident.

For one thing, it happened just days before we were supposed to run off together. That was too much of a coincidence to swallow. But Cassidy was right. There was no smoking gun, no bloody knife, no poison in his system. Nothing but a bloody garage and a case of bad timing.

The bellboy let me into the room—our room. I opened the drapes and looked out at the sparkling ocean. I could feel his arms around me. I had never thought much about the afterlife, but I knew he was in that room, with me, loving me.

Hudson was a formidable man. But even he couldn't cheat death. The bastard tore his head off his body. Yet here I was, daydreaming like a schoolgirl as if I could will him back to life.

I threw myself onto the bed and thought about the last time we were down here.

We had slipped off our clothes. It was too hot, even with the ceiling fan going, for us to crawl under the covers. So we laid there, side by side. Then Hudson picked up a wine bottle which the bellboy had opened for us, and he started at my neck and poured a light stream of wine down my body, between my breasts, between my legs.

I gasped as he slowly licked the wine off my body. I watched the muscles in his arms tense as he lowered himself on top of me. One thing you had to say about my love, he was cut, lean but muscular. I teased him; it was my turn to take a drink. But he couldn't wait. He lowered himself into me, and it was far more than the joining of two bodies. Our hearts, our minds, and our souls melded. I couldn't tell where I stopped and he began.

When it was all over, we walked onto the terrace, still naked. Our room had complete privacy so we felt free to throw off any remnants of our lives outside this paradise.

Also, this gave him a chance to admire my physique. At thirty years old, I didn't have to fight against time yet, but that didn't keep me from working out. I was fanatical about staying in shape…just the way I was fanatical about being in love.

But that was all in the past. I shook my head to clear it. I had to stay present and focused. I got up, took a cold shower, threw on my bathing suit, and went for a walk on the beach. I walked until the sun went down.

My head was clearer. I realized I had to stop idolizing Hudson in death. He wasn't a perfect man. On occasion, he'd stood me up with no explanation. I rationalized it by assuming that kind of thing came with the adultery territory. He had a company to run, a wife, a daughter. I was philosophical about it all…until our pleasant little affair turned to one of desperate love. We both felt the same way. What had started as casual turned to life-changing. I had to have him, the good with the bad. I knew he wasn't a perfect man, but I loved him anyway.

And now my life seemed to drift without purpose. He was gone. Staring at the Mexican sunset, I couldn't envision life without him. It was the first time I contemplated suicide.

Back at my room, I called Cassidy. "I think I'm going mad. I can't let it go. I'm going to dig some more into your father's death."

Cassidy was growing impatient with me. She wanted closure and I was hounding her, keeping her from moving on with her life. I know I was being selfish but couldn't help it. I begged her to do one thing to help me. Since there would never be any forensic evidence to prove that Vivian had something to do with Hudson's murder, they'd have to get a confession out of her.

Cassidy's laugh was harsh. How were they going to do that?

I had an idea.

CRYSTAL

June 17

13

I WAS JUST LEAVING MY PRE-NATAL yoga class. I was on top of the world. I loved being pregnant, knowing a new life was growing inside me. It made me feel special. I had no illusions about Jonathan. He wanted a boy but would ignore him and me about a month after the birth. But all that trouble paled in comparison to the love I felt welling up inside me. I'd never experienced anything like that before. I was going to be a mommy. I was going to have a child who would nurse at my breast and cling to me and love me unconditionally. I couldn't wait.

I got into the car and fully intended to go straight home and take a nap when I passed the most adorable baby store. The strollers, bassinets, toys, breast pumps, rattles, and stuffed animals beckoned. I hadn't really shopped for this baby yet. It seemed like a good time to start.

I went into the store and made my rounds, the clerk following behind me, basket in hand. I quickly filled the basket, and we switched to a cart as I grabbed anything that struck my fancy.

As I got to the counter and handed over my American Express, I was on top of the world. So much of my life had gone wrong. This miracle was going to make up for everything.

Then I felt it. At first, just a twinge in my abdomen. The doctor had warned me to expect odd pains as my uterus expanded and my stomach grew. But by the time I got to the car, the pain had grown. It doubled me over. All my packages fell to the ground, and the last thing I remember before passing out was the alarmed clerk running out of the store to help me.

The pain seemed like it was cutting me in two as I woke up in the hospital. I looked around confused having no idea what happened. A nurse came over and looked down on me with pity. I asked her what had happened. She said she was under orders that the doctor was to be the first to talk to me. She went back to the nurse's desk and ordered my OB-GYN paged. Then the nurse came over to take my vitals. I told her I was in pain, and she said she'd give me something for it. As she pushed some medication into my I.V., I asked about my baby. Was he okay? Did I just faint?

Dr. Stewart showed up. He had been my doctor since I'd started fertility treatments over a year ago, and we had bonded. He had tears in his eyes when he said, "I'm so sorry. I know how much you wanted this baby. You had a spontaneous miscarriage." Tears streamed down my cheeks as I asked if it would be that way with every baby.

The doctor sadly nodded, "Probably." But before he could say more, Jonathan came storming in. One of the nurses tried to stop him, but he pushed right passed her.

He gave me a disgusted look, then turned to the doctor, "Did you tell her?"

The doctor wasn't about to take shit from Jonathan or anyone else. "Some of it. I was about to tell her the rest when you barged in here. This is the recovery room. Only patients and staff allowed back here." Dr. Stewart wasted no time in calling security. He knew Jonathan thought rules were for everyone else.

Jonathan leaned down to me. I could smell the booze on his breath. For half a second I thought he might embrace me or comfort me in some way. Instead, he grabbed my shoulders and jerked me up to sitting position. I screamed in pain. Neither the doctor nor the nearby attending nurse could get him off me. He practically growled, "I should have known you'd fail me. I want you out of my house and out of my life."

By then the security guards arrived and pulled him out of the room. He was still screaming his hatred for me and how I'd failed him. When he was gone, I asked the doctor what Jonathan was talking about when he said, "sliced and diced." The pain medication started to kick in and I felt woozy as the doctor gently told me they had to do a D and C. It was a fairly simple procedure. There would be blood and pain afterwards, but not for long. As I let this sink in, I could see there was more. The doctor told me carrying a baby to term was most likely not going to happen for me. I couldn't take in the words. Not only had I lost this baby but also the chance for any more babies. I think the grief would have killed me but the drugs knocked me out first.

I woke up a few hours later to find I'd been moved to a regular room. My thoughts were like fog in a forest. I could see the trees out my window, but just barely. Slowly the fog lifted and my memory came back strong. My baby was dead. And there would be no more. I don't know if it was the drugs or the shock of it all, but I didn't cry this time. I didn't react at all. I reached for feelings of bereavement but felt nothing.

I rang for the nurse and asked if I could be discharged. The shocked nurse said she would consult with my doctor. I started to look around for my clothes.

Dr. Stewart rushed in. He must have been merely steps away. It touched my heart that someone so busy would wait around for me to wake up. He wasn't interested in hearing my request to be released. I needed rest. There was still bleeding and he wanted to keep me overnight. I robotically said no. I'm going home. I think the lack of emotion in my voice worried him more than if I'd been hysterical. He knew Jonathan, and he was more worried about what would happen to me once I got home. I nodded and told him I'd be a good little girl. I could tell he wanted to stay and somehow counsel me but he was paged, and both he and the nurse left the room.

I immediately tore out my I.V. and ripped off my gown. I found my dress, which had some blood on it. But I didn't care. I had to get out of there. Still running on autopilot, I got dressed, found my purse, and snuck out a back door. Then I used my cell to call a cab since I'd left my car at the baby store and certainly was in no condition to drive.

The taxi let me out at my front door. I saw an unfamiliar car in the driveway. I was very stealthy opening the door and climbing the stairs. My pain meds were starting to wear off and I felt excruciating pain but kept going until I got to the partially open door of my bedroom.

I could hear them before I saw them. Sickening guttural noises both male and female coming from the bed. I pushed the door open and saw Jonathan in the middle of intercourse with some young blonde. The girl was alerted to my presence and she stopped, but Jonathan seemed delighted that I was there and told the woman to keep going. Being watched would only enhance his pleasure.

I stood frozen on the threshold of the bedroom until both had climaxed. Before either of them could regain normal breathing, Jonathan reached in his nightstand drawer and drew out a thousand dollars, which he gave to the blonde. He told her to get dressed and get lost—which she did. Then it was just Jonathan and me, alone. He told me he would have asked me to join them in a fun little three-way, but he knew Dr. Stewart wouldn't approve. Too bad. It would have been fun to have one more romp in the hay before I made my permanent exit.

I didn't move. I didn't say anything. My lack of emotion or expression started to unnerve Jonathan and his temper rose. He yelled at me to get out of there. He was expecting another lady caller soon, and he wanted to take a little nap before she got there. All total, he planned on entertaining four beautiful women during the course of the day and night to celebrate his freedom from the ball and chain of his wife, the useless woman.

I finally spoke. I woodenly told him I would use the bathroom, grab some clothes, and be out of there right away. His response was to turn on his side and immediately start snoring.

I went into the bathroom. There was more blood on my dress. I stared at myself in the mirror without blinking. Then, I looked around the bathroom wondering what to pack.

My eyes fell on the prescription bottle. Viagra. I opened it. It was about half empty.

I didn't form a plan or a strategy or idea. I didn't have enough emotional, physical, or mental energy to do any of those things. I continued to be on autopilot. I poured five or six pills out of the bottle into my palm. I used the bottom of my hairbrush to break the pills into little pieces. I worked until they were little more than grains. Then, I put them in a glass of water and stirred until they were fully dissolved.

Before Jonathan woke up, I ran into the bedroom and switched my glass of water with the one he always kept on his nightstand. He was so drunk, I didn't think he'd notice if the water tasted different.

Then, the doorbell rang. I struggled to run back to the bathroom and closed the door behind me. I fell to the floor of the bathroom. By then, I was bleeding all over the place but I wasn't about to let Jonathan know I was in there, and I prayed his whore didn't need to use the bathroom. The doorbell rang yet again. I heard Jonathan snort then make his disgusting animal waking noises. He yelled for "Kelly" to let herself in. He saw the water and drank it, as I knew he would.

Kelly came in and stripped for Jonathan. The usual foreplay was short-lived but still long enough to sicken me. How could this man be such a pig? She barely had time to crawl on top of him before he grabbed his chest. Kelly wasn't the brightest star on the horizon and at first, she just thought it was foreplay of some sort.

Jonathan grabbed his crotch and screamed in pain. Kelly told Jonathan she didn't know what kind of game he was playing but it wasn't her thing. She opened the nightstand drawer, took out a wad of cash, and left. Jonathan was still screaming. He rolled around on the bed so violently, he fell on the floor. Then he was silent, seemingly unconscious. I crawled out of the bathroom and went to check his pulse. He was dead.

So there I was, sitting in a pool of my own blood with my dead husband. I figured it was time to dial 911.

MORGAN

June 17

14

MADELYN AND I WERE WAITING OUTSIDE the Amhurst home. I wanted to go in, but my daughter, Maddie, couldn't stop crying, and her hysterics weren't what I needed from my daughter right now.

"Madelyn, please pull yourself together. You'll be no good to Crystal like this. She needs to feel our strength."

"But I can't. It's all too much."

I wanted to freak out too, but my daughter was looking to me for strength. "Remember how we supported Cassidy after she lost her dad? She and Vivian really leaned on us."

"But I hardly know Crystal. She's your friend. And I didn't know Jonathan at all. Not really. I mean, it's sad and everything, but there's nothing I can do to help. Let me go home. You go in there by yourself."

"Of course you know Crystal. She's been through two terrible tragedies in one day. You know she wanted to have a baby more than anything. That's never going to happen. And then, on top of that, she came home and found Jonathan dead on the floor of their bedroom. This is beyond… well, anything. Come on. Pull yourself together and let's go."

I opened the car door and prayed my expression displayed courage. I didn't feel brave. I was horrified for Crystal. What was I going to say? How could there be any way to come back from something like this?

Vivian opened the front door. Dorothy and Anjelica were already there, as was Vivian's daughter, Cassidy. Madelyn was drawn towards Cassidy and Alana.

I hugged Crystal tightly. "I'm so sorry, Darling. What a horrible tragedy."

Crystal was leaning back on the sofa. She had absolutely no expression on her face. She looked like a robot. "It's all right. It's over. It's all over."

Anjelica pulled me aside. She whispered in my ear, "She's been like this all evening. She hasn't shed a tear, hasn't said anything except that one sentence, 'It's over, it's over'."

Lisa flew through the door without knocking. Dorothy came from the kitchen with some broth.

Lisa grabbed me, "What's going on? She lost the baby? Why didn't someone call?"

"No one knew for a while. After the miscarriage, she just left the hospital against doctor's orders. From what I understand, she took a taxi home. A taxi! In her condition. That was…um…this afternoon, I guess. Jonathan died a few hours ago."

Anjelica filled us in as best she could. She had found them at home, in their bedroom. Right before the paramedics showed up, she had come over to visit. She'd called a couple of times first and hadn't gotten an answer. She had seen a taxi outside the house and thought something was off, so she went over and knocked on the door. Nothing. It wasn't locked, so she just let herself in. Crystal was sitting next to Jonathan on the floor. He wasn't moving. Blood was everywhere, but it wasn't coming from Jonathan. It was coming from Crystal. Anjelica had panicked, felt for Jonathan's pulse, and tried to get a reaction from Crystal who was clearly conscious but expressionless and motionless. That was hours ago. Anjelica wiped tears from her eyes, "She just keeps repeating 'It's over.'"

I was confused and heartbroken. I turned and whispered quietly to Anjelica, "Does she mean the pregnancy? The chance to have another baby? Is she talking about her marriage? Jonathan's life? What did she mean?"

Dorothy left the broth untouched on the side table and came to join us. "No one knows, and everyone is too afraid to ask. I asked her if she wanted us to leave, and she said no. She's been holding tightly to Vivian's hand. Viv's presence seems to be of some special comfort to her. Maybe it's because she just lost her husband too. I don't know."

The side door flew open and James and Zac came dashing in. Cassidy melted into a puddle. Alana and Madelyn threw their arms around her as she sobbed, "So much death. Again..."

Vivian was sitting next to Crystal on the bed, holding her hand, but her instinct was to fly to Cassidy's side. James saw her concern and swore that the five kids would take care of each other. They exited en masse.

Anjelica looked at the time. It was getting late. But none of us wanted to leave, and Crystal certainly couldn't be left alone. I know I'm not known for being the kindest or sweetest of the bunch. I was cold and calculating and selfish and nothing was more important to me than me. I actually dreamed about handbags and shoes. I mean, who dreams about accessories? I had no illusions. I was known for being Morgan the Bitch. I'd been a bad mother to Maddie and a terrible stepmother to James. My excuse had always been that I was doing my best in a bad situation. Sheraton was a horrible husband. If I was a cold cup of water, he was ice. Whatever affection or love we ever felt for each other had long vanished. We stayed together more out of habit and pretense than anything else.

But in this moment, watching Crystal's frozen expression, clutching Vivian's hand so hard it was turning red, something changed in me. I knelt down in front of Crystal and said, "Wait a minute. Let's stay with Crystal...all night."

15

DOTTY COULDN'T STAY SINCE TOMMY SEEMED to be running a fever at home, so it was just the four of us girls taking care of Crystal. She was in comfy PJ's and a robe, reclining on the sofa. All of the Ladies were surrounding her, devastation on their faces but lacking meaningful words of comfort. They knew anything they said would be trite in light of her condition. But we knew she needed us, so we sat in silence until I decided we needed to take our minds off our present situation.

"How many nightgowns do you have?" My question seemed to jolt her out of her semi-coma state.

"How many what?"

I couldn't believe what I was about to say. "We're spending the night. We're not leaving your side until you're in better condition. No matter how long it takes. We won't leave."

I looked around the room at all my best friends, and they looked at me as if I were from outer space. Lisa brought me a very large glass of scotch, "Are you out of your mind?"

Anjelica burst out laughing. Then she held her hand over her mouth. "I'm so sorry. It's just that Morgan, of all people to suggest that we band together when we all know…"

"I'm not Ms. Warm-and-Fuzzy. But I watched the kids leave the house earlier and saw the closeness between them. As hard as we've tried to screw them up, they are loyal and would take a bullet for their friends. And shitty things have happened. We need to take a page out of our kids' book and band together…hold tightly to each other and never let go. And if I, the coldest ice queen of all, have turned to mush and that's funny, well then, go ahead and make fun of me. I think we could all use a good laugh."

Anjelica threw her head back and actually chortled. Then they all started giggling. Lisa, Vivian, and finally even Crystal, who let go of Vivian's hand long enough to throw her arms around me and say, "Holy fuck, what a weird-ass slumber party this is going to be!"

It *was* the strangest slumber party in the recorded history of women. It turned out that Crystal had more, and more varied types of night attire than any other woman in the world. She didn't wear any of the fancy ones, of course. She lay back on the sofa in a comfy robe and watched the rest of us parade around in her sexy lingerie. She had everything from fleecy comfy PJ's to sexy black baby dolls complete with crotchless panties. I don't know what came over us, but we each picked a different outfit and started drinking. We took a lot of Polaroid pictures that night. I think they ended up in a safe in Crystal's library. I hope nobody sees them but if they do, the hell with it. I looked damn good in that pink, see-through kimono.

We spilled our guts to each other that night. We thought we knew each other well, but there were deep dark secrets that came to light that night. Like the fact that Lisa lost her virginity at the age of fourteen to the quarterback of the junior high school football team and was quite the slut in high school. I was drunk enough to ask her why the hell did she marry Carson? Everyone knew Carson ran Lisa's household. Ran her life. She was practically a slave to the man.

Lisa took a deep sip of her wine and poured another glass as she said, "It wasn't that way in the beginning. But after the wedding, I saw how things really were with Carson. And then the kids came to live with us and he started to treat me like a servant. It's all but over with us. I can't sponge off my mother. I have no skills, never went to college. Our prenup is tight. If we divorce, I don't get a dime.

"I worked so hard designing that house. I picked out every tile, every wall color, every piece of décor. I love that house. And I'll have to leave, move back to my hideous home town, and pour drinks for a living.

"We were poor when I was growing up, but I had the love of my mom and stepdad. Now I'll have nothing. He's leaving me with nothing. How could I be so stupid?"

Lisa fought tears. She pushed me away, assuring everyone she'd be fine; this was Crystal's night. We had to focus on her.

But Crystal said it made her feel good that her friends felt safe enough to share their sorrows too. She wanted everyone to have a chance to talk, to commiserate.

Anjelica admitted she grew up quite poor too, only her life began in a Mexican village just south of Merida. She was raped when she was twelve. She beat the man with a shovel, actually whacked the attacker on the side of his head. But he eventually overpowered her. As she told the story, you could see she could still feel the trauma as if it happened yesterday. The man turned out to be Anjelica's uncle, and Anjelica had to flee to Mexico City. The rape had been especially brutal and violent. It took a long time to recover physically. She had never recovered mentally. She crossed the border illegally and got a job waiting tables in San Diego. That's where she met Alphonse. She fell in love with him instantly. She had seen him in movies before and couldn't believe her luck…that a famous actor would be attracted to her. She told him the truth about her situation and he, since he had become an American citizen years before to avoid British taxes, already had all the connections needed to help Anjelica gain U.S. citizenship. They were married soon after.

Vivian knew most of them had heard her story. Before she met Hudson, she was climbing up the ladder of success in the world of academia. She had a bachelor's degree in physics and two masters, one in Computer Science and one in Corporate Security with an emphasis on Information Technologies. He married her so he would be taken seriously. She married him because she loved him. Their sex life had been pretty much non-existent. Although he played the dutiful husband in public, he was like a stranger in private. He became a little softer when his first wife died. She saw a gentle side of him. But that didn't last long. She should have seen it coming...the affairs...the abandonment. She was caught up in their little world of Avalon. She loved this world. It was home to her. And these women were her family.

Lisa asked her what she was planning on doing. Vivian surprised us all by floating the idea of her taking Hudson's position as CEO of the company. She was certainly qualified. The board would fight her on it. But she was anxious to get back to work so...they'd just have to wait and see.

Everyone then turned and looked at me. Crystal said, "Your turn, Morgan. This party was your idea. Spill."

My story was boring, even to my own ears, but I told it. I had been Miss Howdy-Do-Texas when Sheraton met me. The competition took place on one of his docked cruise ships, so he had been invited to be a judge. I always meant to go to college, but I entered my first pageant in high school and I won. So I entered another and won...and I just kept winning. I guess that's why I'd been the last to warm up to the Ladies. I'd always competed with women. I didn't know you could ally yourself with them, until now.

The rest of my story was predictable. After the pageant, Sheraton sent a note to me backstage saying he would like to meet me, and the rest is history. He wined and dined me and I loved him, not because he was rich...well, partly because he was rich. But also because he treated me like a queen. I think we actually made love once with me wearing just my tiara. Then he tried it on, and it looked just ridiculous and we laughed and made love again. He was so happy with me back then.

Now…I can't remember the last time we made love. And he seems to call on my pageant skills more and more, like he's trotting me out in public as if I'm Miss Howdy-Do-Texas all over again.

Anjelica piped up, "Honey, we're all trophy wives. Let's face it."

I shook my head. "At least I'm good at something."

Anjelica shot a worried look over to Crystal and observed that maybe this party was getting too serious. She thought we needed to liven it back up. She had an idea. She whispered something in Crystal's ear. Crystal whispered something back, and Anjelica ran upstairs and brought down a plastic tiara. Apparently, Crystal had been homecoming queen at her high school, and she kept this in a box in her closet.

And since I had been a real pageant queen, everyone demanded I wear it and I did. I did my walk, my wave, my speech on world peace, the whole thing. Soon we realized the sun was coming up, and we had to get home. We left feeling better, with smiles on our faces. Most of all, Crystal seemed to feel better. It had felt good to laugh.

16

THREE DAYS LATER, THE LAUGHTER WAS all over. Jonathan's autopsy results came in, and they were as startling as they were embarrassing. I was sitting at the dinner table with Sheraton, James, and Madelyn. Silverware scraping against the plates as we cut steak, took sips of wine, and did a little chewing. There were no other sounds in the house. We were not one of those families who chatted about our day. I happened to know that James had won a very important debate for the school's team that day but no one dared mention it to Sheraton. He had made it very clear that what the children did at school was expected to be excellent, always A's, always perfect. So for them to come home and announce that they'd scored a touchdown or won some academic award would be boring.

The sound of the phone ringing broke the silence and made us all jump. No one used the landline in our house. Everyone was always on their cells. The only reason they kept the damn thing in the hallway was because it looked a bit like an antique. It kept ringing. We waited for one of the servants to pick up, but no one did.

Finally, Sheraton got up. "God damn it." He threw his napkin down and he went to the phone, "What?" He listened for a moment before clearly interrupting the person on the other end of the phone. "We're having dinner now. This is family time. Don't you girls yack enough during the day? Call back later."

He hung up. My sick sense of humor was awakened by my husband's talk about the sanctity of their precious family time. I looked over at Madelyn and James, and they must have had the same thought because they were choking food into their napkins.

Trying not to sound too anxious, I asked, "Who was that, Darling?"

"Crystal."

My blood went cold. "Sheraton, you know what Crystal's just been through. My cell phone is dead and needs to be charged. I don't think she called to interrupt dinner, but it must have been important. I've got to find out what it is." Sheraton stood up, "Cook worked very hard on this dinner. You can leave after you've finished it."

I picked my steak up on my fork, walked to the back door, and threw the damn thing in the lake. Then I turned back to my husband, "I'm done now." And I walked out.

I met Anjelica, Lisa, and Vivian, in the middle of the street, all called by Crystal in the middle of dinner. It was bedlam. Everyone was talking at once, grabbing each other by the shoulders. No one knew anything except that Crystal had called each of them and that it had something to do with Jonathan's death.

Holding hands, we ran across the lawns of four houses and hopped over two white picket fences like we were jackrabbits. Anjelica stepped in some mud and didn't even complain that she'd just ruined her new Jimmy Choos. We got to the front door to find it wide open, waiting for us, Crystal standing in the hallway with a glass of champagne in her hand and a bottle of Dom on ice. Her color was back. She actually looked healthy. She was calm. She was restrained. In fact, there was a bit of a smirk to her. She passed out glasses and poured them to the rim. Then she lifted her glass and said, "Night before last, the five of you stayed with me until sunrise. You kept me alive. I really don't think I could have made it through the night. You told me your stories. And you think you know mine. But not all of it. As most of you know, for so long I've been wanting a baby. I lost track how many times I was inseminated. It never worked. Then finally…the pee turned the stick blue and that was it! I was pregnant. Jonathan was so proud. I told him to hold off on the party at the club. But he took one look at that early detection pregnancy stick and had to make the big announcement. I was finally going to have my baby. He was sure he was going to have his son and all the meanness and tension would go away, and we would finally have a male heir.

"But, as you all know it wasn't meant to be. At the hospital, Jonathan came rushing in, grabbed my arms, pulled me up off the bed, and started shaking me. He said I wasn't a woman anymore. He wanted nothing to do with me. Then he stormed out. I went cold. It was like, when my baby died, part of me died. I went home.

"I found Jonathan in my bed with another woman. She seemed to be a little uncomfortable with me watching them, but he just kept right at it, thrusting away. I couldn't stop staring. I just stood there. It was like my feet had been glued to the floor. I didn't move, even after Jonathan finished and he rolled off the woman, who couldn't wait to grab her clothes and money and get the hell out of there.

"Jonathan informed me he was having a sex marathon to celebrate the dissolution of our marriage.

"I started to feel weak. I was still bleeding. I went to the bathroom and saw his bottle of Viagra. I dissolved some pills in his water. I don't remember how many, but it was too many. Then, I heard the doorbell. I stayed in the bathroom while that bastard started fucking another girl… after drinking his water. It wasn't long before he started groaning in pain. He grabbed his heart then grabbed his crotch. I watched through the bathroom door which I had kept ajar. I watched as my husband rolled off the bed. I knew he was dead."

None of us moved a muscle. The world was spinning. Another death. Another husband. Another bizarre way to die.

Crystal faltered, then found her voice again. "The coroner's office called to tell me that my husband had died of a heart attack due to an overdose of Viagra. The police will do a brief investigation, but the D.A. says they already know Jonathan was visited by three prostitutes that day. It only stands to reason he would take Viagra before each encounter. Everyone knows Jonathan didn't like to fail at anything. So I used my husband's reputation against him. I killed my husband. I still can't believe I did that. When I was grinding up those pills, I didn't have a thought in my head. It was like I was outside watching myself. I was so hurt. I had wanted to make him so happy. I had loved him so much. I know we were an odd match. He was so much older than me. I guess I have father issues or something. I don't know. I just know I loved a man who treated me like dirt. I'll never do that again. You women now know the truth. Please don't tell Dorothy or anyone. Please don't make me go to jail."

We grabbed tightly onto Crystal, saying we wished we'd been the ones to put those pills in his water.

It was strange to watch Crystal change before our very eyes. She'd always been the quiet one, so sweet and innocent. But the woman who stood before us was a warrior, and she had won the battle. She shook her head, saying she wished she could feel remorse, but she just couldn't. "Jonathan was a horny, mean son of a bitch, and I'm glad he's dead."

JAMES

June 27

17

JONATHAN'S FUNERAL WAS THE POLAR OPPOSITE from Hudson's. Both men had died in provocative and absurd ways. And while there were a lot of whispers and shocked reactions about the violent and seemingly random decapitation at Hudson's funeral, there was also a sense of at least a little sadness. The eulogies had been meaningful and heartfelt. The tears real. I was no exception. I had always caddied for Hudson during the yearly club tournament. He was a scratch golfer, but never could put together a great eighteen holes during the country club's annual tournament to beat Jonathan. Jonathan was older, but he had nothing but time on his hands, so he played all the time, hired the best pros to teach him, and he was unstoppable. He was also a complete dickhead.

I only showed up today because my dad insisted I go. I had no idea what my dad saw in Jonathan. I was proud of my dad. Sheraton

Firestone was self-made. He worked hard. He married my mom when they were both on full-ride scholarships at Purdue University. He had a dream, and that dream turned into a fleet of luxury cruise liners. They were scattered all over the world. But the dream came at a price. Dad became a workaholic. All that work took a toll on my parents' marriage, and they divorced before my first birthday. He waited all of six months before he married my stepmom, Morgan, and she popped out a baby nine months later—Madelyn.

I thought of Maddie as more of a friend than a sister. But we were close. I was shuffled back and forth between my mom and my dad for years, so it wasn't always easy for me to fit in with the club babies. But lately my mom had been spending more time in Spain sleeping with some guy who made wine or something…I didn't know him, didn't care to. I was glad to live with my dad. Morgan was a cool stepmother, and I could be with my friends.

I scanned the crowd, a little smaller than Hudson's service. Not a wet eye in the house. My stepmom was sitting with the widow, Crystal. I really liked her. Crystal was bomb. She always treated us kids like adults. She never talked down to us, and she made sure we always felt included in fun club activities, like sand volleyball tournaments, and was instrumental in having a basketball court put in the back of the property. I often wondered why she married such a tool, and now, as I studied her face, I saw no expression of grief or pain. In fact, as I eyed the whole pew of women, they all seemed a little…well, it wouldn't be quite accurate to say they were lighthearted, but considering they were at a funeral, they seemed calm…like they'd been through a storm and the worst was over. The Ladies spoke softly and shared slight nods and hugs. I leaned forward to listen and heard them discuss their plans for the memorial luncheon afterwards. Their whispers had a bit of a lilt, as if they were looking forward to getting through the ceremony and onto what could only be called a party.

Cassidy was sitting with her stepmom. She seemed a little more subdued than anyone else. And why wouldn't she? This had to remind her of her father's death. I then looked over at Alana. She looked bored and was actually Instagramming on her phone.

Carson sat with Sheraton and Alphonse since their wives were on the other side of the aisle forming a wall of protection around Crystal.

As the minister got up to speak, there was a bit of a commotion in the back. We all turned to see Tommy and Dorothy coming in late. Dorothy joined the women, and Tommy went to sit with his buds. Zac, their son, went to sit with Cassidy. I know nothing romantic had happened between Zac and Cassidy, but there was something there. I think they really loved each other. There had been so much crap going on, they didn't know it. I was looking forward to the time they just admitted they were hot for each other and moved into something more serious.

They were all enjoying their last summer together before starting college. Maddie and Alana had decided to join me at Santa Monica College. But both Zac and Cassidy had been accepted at Oregon State. I figured, since they were going to the same college, it was just a matter of time.

The eulogy given by the minister couldn't have been more generic. Of course, there were a lot of truths about Jonathan, which needed to be avoided if Jonathan was going to come across as a semi-decent guy. So the fact that he divorced his first wife while she was pregnant the minute the sonogram showed it was a girl was not mentioned. In fact, now that I noticed it, his daughter, Jessica, her husband, Charles, and their baby, Alison, were nowhere in sight.

The minister asked if anyone wanted to speak. The silence spoke volumes. Finally, Tommy got up and said, "I owed Jonathan a lot. Uh…I guess that's all I have to say. Oh, and also he was a good golfer."

Tommy hurried back to his seat and received pats on his back for doing what none of the other guys were willing to do.

The whole service took about ten minutes, and then everyone practically sprinted to their cars and sped to the club.

We club babies did our usual thing, met up in our private spot behind the clubhouse. I had a bottle of JW Black, and Zac had three joints of some really good shit. We lit up and drank. We didn't really talk. There wasn't much to say. Finally, after the scotch and weed kicked in, Alana said, "I get the feeling no one's very sad Jonathan is dead."

We looked through the clubhouse windows at the gathering inside. People were laughing, eating, and chatting as if they were celebrating. The men were watching a baseball game on the TV, and the women were arguing about whether or not Anjelica should cut her hair.

It was so surreal, so crazy. A really rich and powerful man just died, and his "friends" were partying like it was New Year's Eve. I pointed out the obvious to my buds, "The guy was a douche. He was mean to his wife...the nicest lady in the world. He never worked a day in his life. So I figure the world's a better place without him."

The others nodded, then we decided to drive to the nearest 7-Eleven. We were too stoned to eat the posh finger food being passed around in the club. And there's no better way to say goodbye to such a dick than with a six-pack of Monster and a giant bag of Flamin' Hot Cheetos.

18

THE PHONE WOKE ME UP AT eleven a.m., and I was pissed. Everyone knows I'm not a morning person and can barely function before noon. Half the time, I miss my first two periods at school, but my dad would just write a note and everything would be fine. Everyone bows to Sheraton Firestone because he's always giving away free cruise tickets. The phone call was from Zac. He sounded a little panicked and asked me to come over right away. I jumped into some board shorts and flip-flops and ran three houses down. There was a car parked in front. It didn't look familiar. The Nolans had visitors, and from the sound of Zac's voice, it wasn't welcome company.

I hurled myself into the living room to find Tommy, Dorothy, Zac, and some stranger. I apologized. Was I interrupting?

The guy was wearing a black suit straight off the racks at K-Mart.

He stood, shook my hand, and introduced himself as Detective Shaun Daniels. I demanded to know why he was here. I thought maybe Zac had been busted for weed or something, but I was clearly on the wrong track when Dorothy told me to sit down and be quiet. The detective picked up his line of questioning. Apparently, Tommy owed Jonathan quite a bit of money at the time of his death, and not only was it specified in his will that the debt be forgiven, but that Tommy would inherit $100,000. That would have been a pittance to Jonathan, but it meant a lot to Tommy.

I still didn't understand why a cop was here shaking down the Nolans. Was it a crime to inherit money from a friend? The detective explained that he was just doing a routine investigation. He knew about the three women Jonathan had sex with the day he died. He also knew how old Jonathan was. So the fact that he might have gotten a little carried away with Viagra and had a heart attack was not out of the question. But it's a drug few people O.D. on, so the police just want to look into it a little. Tommy was in debt to Jonathan and stood to gain if he died. Kind of sounds like he had a bit of a motive.

Tommy jumped up. "To kill my friend?"

Dorothy was equally outraged. "Never. You investigate all you want, Mr. Policeman but you'll come up with nothing…nothing but the truth, which is that Jonathan was a sex addict. We loved him but he overdid everything. If you'd known him, you would know it wasn't out of character—the way he died, I mean."

Zac grabbed his mom and had her sit down and be quiet. Her indignation wasn't making this any better. Zac then turned to Daniels and asked, "Are you saying my father killed Jonathan over money?"

Daniels answered quickly, "Not just money. A lot of money. Your father owed him $300,000."

Dorothy and Zac choked. They clearly had no idea. They turned their anger on to Tommy.

Dorothy grabbed her husband by the shoulders, "How could you do that? How did you ever expect to pay him back?"

Tommy looked like a beaten dog. "I thought I'd get on a lucky streak. You know, at the track or in Vegas."

Then Tommy turned to Daniels, "And I had no idea he had it in his will to forgive that debt, let alone leave me money. Ask his lawyer. There goes my motive, right up your ass."

Daniels stepped away. "Okay, everyone calm down. I'm just doing my job, and my job is to ask questions and follow leads. I'm not accusing anyone here, not arresting anyone. I just have to dot my i's and cross my t's. I've asked a lot of questions about Jonathan Amhurst. I spoke with several of his employees and acquaintances. I agree that he probably lost track of how many pills he took that day. But deliberate poisoning has to be considered."

I got a bit defensive, "You talked to his wife?"

"Not yet. But I will."

"She's a good person, she worshiped Jonathan even though he was a bastard through and through..."

Daniels cut me off, "James, I'm sure she's a saint. But I have to talk to her. Don't worry. I'm sure this will all work out."

He got his coat and headed for the door, but before he left, he turned to us and said, "Don't any of you find it odd that two good friends, neighbors, club mates, should die so closely together?"

Dorothy was quick to respond, "Accidents. Both of them. Our little community has had a run of bad luck, that's all."

Daniels put on his coat. "We closed Hudson Montgomery's case. We're about to close this one. I never said they weren't accidents. I said it was odd. And the fact that you don't find it odd is odd." And he turned and left.

19

I WAS HAVING PIZZA WITH ZAC, Maddie, Alana, and Cassidy at our favorite Beverly Hills pizzeria and filling them in on the detective's visit to Zac's mom and dad's. Alana and Maddie seemed more interested in their no-cheese gourmet pizzas than they were with what I was saying. For two girls who were constantly dieting, they sure could pack away their grub. But Cassidy was mesmerized, hung on my every word. I no sooner finished my tale when she made some excuse about a dentist appointment and bolted out of the restaurant. Zac started to get on my case for upsetting her. I appreciated how protective he was with her, but how could we possibly avoid not talking about all this batshit, crazy stuff?

Zac wanted to get up and check on her, having not bought the dentist story, but I said, "Let me." If Zac was going to play the part of the boyfriend, he was going to have to step up and be one. Until then,

Cassidy's obvious emotional problems were all equally our concern.

I left the tiny brick-covered restaurant on Santa Monica Boulevard and turned the corner to head down the alley behind the building when I heard Cassidy on the phone. I pulled up short to overhear what she was saying.

"My friend James said a detective from the LAPD paid a visit to some friends of ours. We lost another member of our club in what appeared to be another accident. The detective said he was closing my father's case. If you really think you can get something on my stepmother, you'd better move fast."

I was jolted. Who could Cassidy be talking to? And why was this the first time I was hearing her suspicions about Vivian in Hudson's death? I thought the five of us told each other everything. Cassidy was silent for about a minute as she listened to the mystery person on the other end of the line. Then she responded.

"Tap her cell phone? Clara, are you crazy? Isn't that like seven types of illegal?"

She listened a moment more, then nervously ended the call by saying, "Okay. You get me the chip and I'll put it in her phone. But this is as far as I go. You take it from here." Then I heard her slam her phone into her purse. I timed my turn around the corner so it looked like I'd just gotten there. Still, Cassidy was suspicious and edgy. "What the fuck are you doing? Spying on me?"

"Hell no. Just checking on you. Seemed like my story about the cop upset you. I would never in a million years want to freak you out. I'm sorry. I guess it made you think of your dad dying. I didn't mean to. It was just so ratchet the way the guy didn't really accuse Tommy but acted real suspicious. I guess that's just how cops are."

"I guess. Now, like I said before, I gotta go." She took off for her car, which was parked in the alley. Still clearly upset, she got in her cherry red Audi AR8 and screamed out of the parking lot. What the hell was going on with her? She was conspiring with someone to prove that her stepmom had something to do with her dad's death? I was no Vivian fan, but that sounded way far-fetched. But Cassidy obviously had her doubts, enough to be willing to break the law and put a tap on her stepmom's phone. Who was this Clara person who had access to such equipment? Cassidy was being swayed by someone who was giving her really bad, dangerous advice. Now the question I had to ask myself is, what was I going to do about it?

MADELYN

July 7

20

DON'T YOU HATE THAT FEELING WHEN it's like everyone in the room knows something you don't? That's what it felt like after pizza the other day. We caught up with Cassidy about a week later at her house. She was in her backyard floating on an inflatable raft that could easily fit three people. She was in the middle of her pool on her stomach, her lime green bikini untied in the back. I had always liked her pool. The sheer size of it was impressive. It was as big as a football field, with beautiful yellow and blue tile all around it.

Of course, when it came to pools, no one could match ours. We had to have this over-the-top, extravagant pool, my dad being a cruise liner guy and all. Our pool had all these fountains and jets, a swim-up bar, a waterfall, and next to that was a built-in slide. We never swam at the club, choosing to do our pool lounging privately at our house. Our pool also had a high diving board that no one but my dad ever used. He'd put his Speedos on and do double flips and stuff. It embarrassed the hell out of me and my mom. No girl or wife who doesn't live on the French Riviera wants to see a man in a Speedo, let alone her own father.

But today we found ourselves in Cassidy's backyard. When she heard us come through the back gate uninvited, she wasn't very happy. In fact, she kept floating, saying nothing to us.

We respected her privacy and kept our distance, opting to go to the fully stocked tiki style pool house and fire up the blender, making enough margaritas to last a couple of hours. Zac took off his shirt and pants and jumped in, boxers only, and swam out to Cassidy to give her one. She reached back and tied her top then turned and took the margarita. There were tears in her eyes. She thanked Zac and invited him up onto the raft. They didn't talk. We didn't talk. Finally, Cassidy and Zac were ready to swim back to us. We moved to the fire pit. It was starting to get dark, so Zac turned on the gas and threw a match in the pit. We just drank in silence as the sun went down. Finally, James spoke up, "Don't do anything stupid, Cassidy."

Cassidy glared at him, "What do you think I'm going to do?"

James sat back and looked up at the stars. He just couldn't confront her face to face as he accused, "You're working with some chick named Clara to bug your stepmom's phone. You can't do that, you know."

Ah, I was finally in the loop. I'd been wondering what was going on with Cassidy and James, and from the looks on Zac and Alana's faces, I realized I wasn't the only one unaware. It made me feel better. Anyway, we were talking and being open and honest again.

I had to ask, "What are you gonna do that for?"

Cassidy took a deep breath and decided to confess, "Vivian might have had something to do with my dad's death. I know it sounds strange what with the garage door and all, but I met this woman…she's a reporter. And, while I'm being honest here, she was Dad's mistress. Apparently, Dad was going to leave Viv and after he told her that…well, that's when the accident happened. And maybe it was just an accident, but there's no way my stepmom would have just let my dad go off with another woman. She'd put up a helluva fight. In fact, she did. I heard and saw some of it through my drunken stupor. Anyway, they fight and then he's just dead like that? Clara and I just want to look into it. I just want to know for sure."

Murder. The word choked in our throats. This was a whole new ballgame. However, as we mulled over her connection to this Clara person and the plan they had, we universally arrived at the conclusion that it was probably a wild goose chase. But if anything popped up...we'd be there for her one hundred percent. She was playing a dangerous game. If Vivian found out, God knows what revenge she'd wreak on Cassidy. But Cassidy assured us that was a risk she was willing to take. She loved her dad too much not to be sure. Tears welled in her eyes again as we joined hands and promised Cassidy we wouldn't breathe a word to anyone. When it came time to part, she hugged the guys, then she grabbed onto me and Alana and whispered, "You guys are the best."

I told her I loved her and she smiled through tears, "I love you too, Maddie."

Early the next morning, I woke to the kind of hangover only tequila can give you. I stumbled to our retro 1950s kitchen for coffee and aspirin. I switched on the light and blinked as it bounced off the turquoise and white tile. I turned on the faucet and threw four pills in my mouth. I hated the old-fashioned sink with mirrored backsplash. In fact, our whole house was mid-century, lots of posts and beams and walls of glass—kind of like Frank Lloyd Wright had vomited on the ground and out popped our house. It was the least private house on the lake. While our backyard was stunning, both my mom and I hated the house. But my father loved "classic" themes, and he adored this place.

I heard a sound coming from the family room. It was three in the morning. I went to investigate and came across my mom looking at some photos. The minute she heard me, she stuck them back in an envelope. She was shaking. Her usually perfectly coiffed hair was a rat's nest, and her clothes were covered in gook.

"What the hell happened to you, Mom?"

"Madelyn, watch your language, young lady. And go to bed."

"You're the one who needs to go to bed. You look like shit."

"I was cooking cheesecake."

"Why would you do that? What do you have Antonia for? Let her do her job, the cooking, the cleaning, the…"

"I like to bake a cake every once in a while. My mom taught me. It soothes me, makes me feel close to her. Sometimes I miss her so much."

"Yeah, you look real soothed. Come on, Mom. What's going on? What are those photos?"

"Maddie, this is a private matter, and I'm not going to discuss it with you."

I didn't back off. Instead, I gently nudged her up the stairs, escorting her to bed. She turned and hugged me tightly. "I love you so much. I lost my parents when I was so young. I never wanted you to go through that. I wanted you to have a stable and loving home. I'm sorry I failed."

I laid her gently on top of the bed, the envelope still clutched in her hand. "You can't say things like that if you're not going to tell me the whole story."

"You're right. It will all be fine. You are strong. All the women in my family are strong. That is our gift. That is your gift."

"Have you been drinking tonight, Mom?"

"No."

"Then thanks for the words of encouragement. Now go to sleep. Whatever is wrong, it will all seem better in the morning."

I waited until she closed her eyes then I crossed the room that she shared with my father. I grimaced at the décor. It was the polar opposite of downstairs. My dad always got carried away with themes, and he came home one night and decided to do each of our bedrooms in a special theme. I wouldn't let him touch my bedroom, which was just a regular room with pink paint, a bed, and pictures of my friends on the walls.

But this room got out of control, and there was nothing Mom could do about it. It was all beading, lavender drapes, and ornate teak dressers from Thailand. It looked like the set of a Rudolf Valentino movie. When I was little, I was never one of those girls who wanted to climb into my mom and dad's bed. I think I knew even then it was god-awful tacky. Expensive, but crass as hell.

I went downstairs and waited for a half hour. The longest thirty minutes of my life. Then, I went back up, cracked her bedroom door open, heard her even breathing, and knew she was asleep. I crept through the dark and slowly pulled the envelope out of her hand.

I went down to the kitchen and pulled out the color 8x10 photos. I don't know what I was expecting, but what I got was a punch in the gut.

There were pictures, must have been twenty of them, of my dad...I couldn't tell the locations. In each photo, he was with another man. In some of the pictures, he was in a suit in a nice restaurant clinking glasses of wine with another classy looking guy. Then the next shot was of them kissing on a secluded street corner. Another photo showed my dad in his ever-popular speedo sleeping on the beach with his head resting on the stomach of yet another man. Photo after photo...the message was clear. My dad was living two lives. And the way he looked so happy in the pictures, he obviously preferred men.

I heard the sound of a throat being cleared, and I saw my distraught mother in the doorway. "I should have hid them. I knew you would be too concerned to just let this go. But now do you understand why I never wanted you to see these?"

I needed to back up a little. "How...I mean, why...Who took these?"

"I knew your father was cheating on me. I hired a private detective to follow him. I assumed your dad was fooling around with prostitutes or a dancer from one of his ships or...I didn't know, one of those cute cruise directors. I had no idea...But it explains a lot. We haven't made love in...well, I can't remember how long, that's how long it's been."

"What are you going to do?"

"Divorce, I guess. Unlike my friends, there's no prenup in place, so I'll get half of everything. But this is so not what I wanted...a broken family...a broken marriage."

She started to cry. I didn't know what to feel about my dad. After all, there are two sides to every story. But in that moment my heart broke for my mom, and I hugged her and wouldn't let go until her tears ceased. "So you're going to confront him about this?"

"Yes. I am not cut out for pretense or leading a secret life…hence my nickname, Morgan the Bitch. With me, you get what you see. He did love me once. I know he did. But I don't know how far back this behavior goes. Maybe our entire seventeen years of marriage have been a scam. I raised you alone while he was off enjoying his armada of floating palaces of fantasy and fun. I gave him my energy, my life. And he took it. Damn him."

I had to ask, "Would you feel differently if these were photos of Dad with other women?"

"I probably shouldn't, because cheating is cheating. But his sexuality is something a wife has a right to know. It feels like the lie is so much bigger. I thought I knew my husband. I never knew him at all."

"Me either. I guess I'll have to get to know him all over again. You know I'll have to talk to him about this. I mean, he's still my dad and I love him."

"I know. But let me talk to him first, okay?"

"I promise. Now go back to bed, Mom. We'll sort this out."

21

IT WAS THE CLUB'S FOURTH OF July extravaganza. Members were out in full force. I had wanted to go with my mom, but I hadn't seen her all day. And Dad was finishing up a round of golf with Alana's dad, Alphonse. They were paying their caddy and telling him to put their golf bags on the rack near the lake. My head was swimming. I'm not the type of person who can think of more than one thing at a time. And there I was at this party and all this internal drama was going on with Cassidy wanting to bug her mother's phone and my dad being gay, and I just went all kinds of brain dead.

The kids wanted to join me on the steps overlooking the putting green to watch the fireworks, but I needed to find my mom. Everyone was on one side of the club settling in for the fireworks display the club sponsored every Independence Day, but my mom and dad were nowhere in the crowd. I headed through the dining room and out the other side of the club. I walked down the flagstone steps to the lake. I could hear their voices in the dark. They were trying to whisper but weren't doing a very good job of it. I stepped back into the shadows so my presence wouldn't be detected.

"Why did you even marry me?"

"Because I run a family-friendly business. I've got to maintain an image as a family man."

"So that's all I was to you, an image?"

"I could come up with something clever but I'm just tired of lying. Now you know. Now we can go on with our lives with a little less tension between us. You understand my needs and I understand yours."

"You understand nothing about me. I want to be your wife, in every way. I don't want to live a lie. And who says you can keep your lie? No matter how discreet you are, someday someone else is going to catch you and it's going to be front-page news. My private detective took a lot of those photos in public. You're not being very discreet. Why don't we just quietly divorce and you can live your life any way you choose?"

"If I wanted things that way I'd have made those arrangements a long time ago. We may seem to be living in a new age of enlightenment, but there's still a price to pay for a man of my stature to live an alternative lifestyle. That's just the way it is. You think I like it? I hate it. But I'm not about to tear down the empire it took me a lifetime to build. And you're going along for the ride."

"As your beard? No way in hell."

My dad grabbed Mom's arms and began shaking her. "You can't leave me."

"Watch me."

I couldn't believe my dad was being so horrible to my mom. I ran away as fast as I could. I ran to my house, and like a scared little girl, hid under the covers of my bed.

ANJELICA

July 4

22

RIGHT BEFORE THE FIREWORKS STARTED, VIVIAN and I had dinner in the clubhouse. I had just been telling her about my husband's latest acting gig as a criminal mastermind on CSI. It wasn't much but it kept food on the table. Actually, I was thinking of going back to work myself.

Vivian smiled, "You may not be well educated, Angelica, but you're a genius, and you can work for me any time."

I was stunned by the offer. I didn't know anything about computer microchips. Vivian assured me there were lots of positions for which I would be qualified. Administration, secretarial, public liaison…the list went on and on. I promised to mull it over. Vivian threw her napkin down. She had finished eating and wanted to go watch the fireworks show, but I had just polished off a plate of steak and corn (diet be damned) when I realized I was way too full, and had to walk a little just to try to avoid the inevitable heartburn after I went to bed tonight. I parted ways with Viv and headed down the steps to the lake when I heard voices. They weren't loud but they were angry. I stepped back and hid near a row of golf bags when I recognized it was Sheraton and Morgan. Worried about Morgan, I stayed close by without revealing myself and listened.

It was Sheraton's voice, "I'll keep you from leaving me any way I have to. I'll stop seeing guys. You want sex, baby. I'll give you sex. We made Maddie together, let's have a little repeat performance."

"Get your hands off of me."

"No way. You said you wanted a real marriage. I can only translate that to mean you want me to fuck you. Glad to oblige."

I peered through the bushes and saw him rip at her clothes. She tried to get away. The sight of Sheraton attacking his wife caused an explosion in my brain. Before I even knew what I was doing, I reached down to Sheraton's golf bag and grabbed an eight iron. Before he could see me, I came up from behind him and smashed in the side of his head as hard as I could.

Morgan looked at me in shock. I was still panting, still holding the club. Then she looked down at Sheraton who moaned. He wasn't completely out and most certainly wasn't dead. I dropped the club and stood motionless. Morgan hugged me. I stared at her face with glassy eyes.

"Anjelica, it's okay. I saw what happened. I'll say I did it. It was self-defense. We'll just call the cops and…" Sheraton moaned again. The sound brought me back to life. My rage was so real and so violent that I picked up the club again and was ready to bludgeon him to death. Morgan's hand interrupted my downward swing. It was so surreal. Like a dream. It was as if I was twelve all over again and my uncle was raping me. All that rage I'd held inside me came out. I wanted to beat Sheraton to death for what he was trying to do to Morgan.

Morgan tried to calm me down, "Anjelica, what are you doing?"

"I saw him grabbing you. All I could think about was all those years ago in Merida. How that man raped me and I tried to get away. I wasn't even thinking. Oh Morgan, I'm so sorry."

Morgan held me. "We have to protect you. We can't let the press or anyone else find out about this. You might do okay in court. We know some damn good lawyers, but the scandal would be disastrous."

Sheraton moaned again. He tried to rise to his knees.

I pushed Morgan, "Go home. And remember, the last time you saw your husband, he was alive."

Morgan freaked, "Alive? What are you going to do?"

"Protect you. Now go, before someone comes along."

Morgan made a quick and panicked retreat.

I looked down at Sheraton and I looked over at the lake. And I had a pretty brilliant idea.

I quickly searched through Sheraton's golf bag and found a Swiss Army knife in one of the pockets. I raced over to the volleyball net. I was surprised at how the adrenaline shot through my body, giving me the strength I needed to cut down the damn thing.

Then I raced back to Sheraton who was trying to stand. I picked up the club and whacked him in the chest to knock the wind out of him, and he fell down to his knees. He couldn't talk and could barely draw breath.

I pushed him to the ground and zipped up his golf bag, which I then placed on top of him. I rolled him up in the net, carefully checking every once in a while to make sure no one was around. There were no lights on, and the moon hadn't come up yet.

He was so heavy that I had to kick his body all the way to the dock. I dragged him to the end of the pier and pushed him in. The last thing I saw before he went under was his eyes opening. He wasn't dead yet, but a night at the bottom of the lake would take care of that.

I felt a rush of power surging through my body. It wasn't grown-up Anjelica who killed Sheraton, it was a twelve-year-old girl who was now big enough and strong enough to take care of monsters like him.

I made sure he went all the way to the bottom, out of sight. Then I went home and had the first peaceful night's sleep in many years.

23

MORGAN AND MADELYN BOTH WENT INTO treatment for post-traumatic stress disorder, though they never revealed to their doctors specifically what the trauma was. Anyway, they were heavily medicated and told everyone they had a terrible case of the flu so people would let them alone. They hadn't asked me what had become of Sheraton, and I didn't tell them. Maddie thought her mom had won the argument and her dad had just taken off. But Morgan knew he was dead.

I, on the other hand, was walking on clouds. I finally had closure. When I saved Morgan, it was like I saved myself. I had been locked in a nightmare most of my life—afraid of everything, even sometimes of my own husband, although he gave me no reason to be. But when a man is stronger and does things to you and you're a little girl barely old enough to have started menstruating, it does things to you. After years of therapy, I thought I was better, that I was over the anxiety and the meds were taking care of everything. But the subconscious never forgets. And when I saw what Sheraton was doing to Morgan, I went insane.

After the murder, I realized insane people can act very sane. I was thinking very clearly. There was clean-up to be done. I questioned Morgan. I needed to know everything that had happened leading up to the near-rape. Morgan told me everything, about Sheraton being gay, living two lives, all of it. She was a wreck. She had had no idea, all this time. She'd offered his freedom willingly but he had lived split-in-two for so long, there was no wholeness to Sheraton. If only he'd been true to himself…It made me realize that it didn't matter what ethnicity, religion, or sexual orientation, greed was the destroyer of souls.

I knew the clock was ticking. So I set to work covering my tracks.

Having had my own papers forged to become legal many years ago came in handy. I called a friend of mine, who forged a passport for Sheraton and that friend (who bore a slight resemblance to the real Sheraton) flew, using the fake passport, to Brazil. Then, after forty-eight hours, I had Morgan call the police and file a missing persons report on her husband. The use of the passport came up right away.

My dear friend Delia, who was editor of one of the most popular tabloids in the world, became helpful also. I slipped her one of the photos Morgan had of Sheraton on the beach with another guy, and Delia splashed it all over the front page of her newspaper. The internet picked it up, and soon it was common knowledge that the "King of the High Seas" had left his wife and daughter for another man. Part of me knew I was behaving like a sociopath, without regret or remorse for my behavior. But it was cathartic for me, healing treatment for years of suffering. My wounds and my anger were assuaged. I was free. Or at least I thought I was.

Seventy-two hours after the murder, I was having lunch with Crystal poolside at the club when a gorgeous, very tall man walked up to us. He had broad shoulders and a chiseled face. He had sandy blonde hair cut very short. I would have called Carson right away to get this guy in the movies but that idea went south as soon as I recognized him. Detective Shaun Daniels.

There is definitely an upside to being just a little short of insane. You can act completely calm in the diciest of circumstances. You could never tell that I was unnerved, to say the least, when I shook Daniels' hand and asked him to join us. He didn't want to intrude but he did have a few questions. I told the waiter to bring this gorgeous young man an iced tea and told him to ask me anything he liked.

It had to do with Sheraton, of course. Both Crystal and I expressed outrage at the way he abandoned his family. Crystal's was sincere, mine was feigned. Crystal wondered what the detective was doing here asking about Sheraton. Not one of his friends knew the truth about him. Not even his wife or children. In fact, they were seeking intensive therapy to deal with the tragedy of his abandonment and the double life he'd been living. Daniels understood all that. But in cases like these, it was standard to follow up, make sure there was no stone unturned. He had questioned both Morgan and Madelyn. He didn't get much out of them as they were constantly trying to speak through sobs. Sheraton's son from his first marriage, James, seemed a little more put together. He clearly loved his father. The story about his dad's sexual orientation didn't bother him as much as the fact that his father never told him the truth, and in the end didn't even say "goodbye."

I grew indignant. "James is a wonderful, young man. But his father was an asshole. As for Maddie and Morgan, of course they aren't calm and rational. They're hysterical. Can you blame them?"

Daniels' iced tea arrived. He stirred it. "I don't blame, I don't judge, I just ask questions and get answers."

I looked him dead in the eye, "What questions could there possibly be left to ask? Every sordid detail has been printed and exposed."

Daniels looked at me and didn't blink. "That story about running off to be with his lover? Yeah, well, I'm looking into it, to see if it's all true. While it seems he did board a flight to Brazil several days ago, he seems to have disappeared once he passed through immigration in Rio. Oh, there were a few photos of him in the papers, but no one can even find the photographers who took the photos. I have some buddies in the police force down there. They've looked around. Seems he can't be found."

"Don't you think that was the point of him leaving? To vanish?"

"Maybe. I'd like just a little more to go on."

"Well, it's been in all the papers."

"We don't use tabloids or the Internet as sources. Maybe the story is true. Maybe not. I've interviewed a lot of people about Sheraton Firestone, read up on him too. He doesn't seem like the kind of guy to walk away from an empire he built out of nothing. And he certainly doesn't seem like a man who would just walk away from a fortune."

"People can fool you, Detective. Sheraton fooled all of us for years. He didn't love his first wife, he didn't love his second wife. Maybe he didn't love money quite as much as we all thought he did. Now, if you're through with me, I've got a nail appointment."

I leaned down and kissed Crystal's cheek, then turned and headed for the parking lot, glad to be away from the detective's piercing blue eyes. But I didn't want to leave. Not just yet. I had to be sure Daniels was off the scent. I doubled back and listened through the French doors of the empty bar.

Back at the table, Daniels sipped on his ice tea. Crystal just couldn't believe Sheraton had fooled them all for so long. Another bizarre incident to happen to their friends in such a short period of time.

Daniels finished his drink, "Yeah, that's what I keep thinking. But you let me worry about all that. How are you holding up?"

"I won't lie to you, Detective. I'm glad my husband's dead and I sleep peacefully knowing he's burning in hell."

"So there is some fight in you. I thought I saw strength in your green eyes, but I wasn't sure that day I met you."

"I wasn't at my best, Detective."

"Call me Shaun."

"Why should I do that?"

"I'm not working right now. Your husband's case is officially closed, and I'm just going through the motions with this Firestone thing."

"Well, go easy on Morgan, okay?"

"Okay. Do you find my manner a little rough?"

"No. But you could be, if you wanted to. I've seen strength in your eyes too. I wouldn't want to be a criminal in one of your cases. You seem like the type who always gets his man."

"I have a pretty good track record."

"I'll bet."

"Could we stop talking about me?"

"What do you want to talk about?"

"I was wondering, since your husband's death didn't break your heart, if you're planning on dating any time soon."

"I hadn't thought about it."

"What if I asked you out?"

The question shocked Crystal, and she got up abruptly. "No. Of course not. It would be so inappropriate. I mean, there aren't any rules or anything. I don't know. Let me think about it."

I was glad I'd stayed and overheard the conversation. It was a relief to hear that the cops weren't taking Sheraton's case very seriously. The fact that Detective Gorgeous had a crush on Crystal was not surprising. Men were always falling in love with her. She had always turned them down, always been faithful to Jonathan. But now that Jonathan was gone, I wondered what might happen between Crystal and Detective Daniels…and if we could use it to our advantage.

I came home to find Alphonse cooking. He was making lamb stew. He only did that when he was in a very good mood. I walked into the kitchen and breathed in the unusual smell. I greeted my husband, who lately had been rude, aggressive, and mean to me. He was singing an old Welsh folk ballad. His baritone voice was deep and lovely and his accent pure and beautiful, as if he had just come from his native land. He put his arms around me and began dancing with me.

"What are you doing?"

"Dancing with my wife and cooking."

"Have you lost your mind?"

"No. I'm just in a great state of mind. And now that you're here, you can share in my joy."

"What joy?"

"I'll tell you at dinner. Alana is spending the night with Cassidy, so we have the whole house to ourselves. I'll finish cooking down here and you go up and change into something nice. Wear the black dress I bought you in New York."

Confused, I headed up the stairs while Alphonse went back to his singing and cooking. I should have been happy as I took my shower. To finally see my husband in a good mood and wanting to share it with me…I should have been doing cartwheels. But there was something off about his mood and his dinner invitation. I couldn't put my finger on it but when I came downstairs dressed to the nines in perfect hair and makeup, I was more wary than ever.

The long dining table that was rarely used was set to elegant perfection. The lace tablecloth had been handmade custom for us by some nuns in Ireland. Waterford crystal candlesticks that usually were hidden away in the butler's pantry were lit and in the center of the table.

Two place settings of our finest Limoges were carefully placed, one on each end of the table. This room had always been exclusively used for large family gatherings or dinner parties. The table comfortably sat twelve, so it was ludicrous that he had sat us as far away as possible, as if we were the fucking Duke and Duchess of York. But I went along with it. He politely held out my chair and I sank into it, still confused. Alphonse poured a dark red cabernet into my glass, then one for himself. Then, Alphonse brought out the main course and served me himself. He went to his place setting. If we were going to have a conversation, it wasn't going to be intimate. We'd have to shout.

"Eat up," Alphonse invited me with a grand gesture as if he was the host and I was his guest. I tried to take a bite but it wouldn't go down. My nerves kicked in. I gulped down some wine just to help me swallow the food. I couldn't wait anymore. I had to know.

"Not that this isn't all lovely and thoughtful of you, but what is this all about?"

"We're celebrating your skill."

"My skill?"

"With an eight iron. I never knew you had such a beautiful swing."

I choked on my wine and coughed into my napkin. I put down my glass, as it was shaking in my hand, and tried to steady my voice.

"I don't know what you're talking about. I don't play golf."

"I know. You've found a whole new use for a golf club. Murder."

"I didn't…I mean, I don't know what you're talking about."

"Whacked him with an eight iron, perfect length, weight, perfect choice. And you really put some muscle into it. Remind me to thank that personal trainer of yours for turning you into a stud."

"What the hell are you talking about? Have you started using drugs with your buddies on the set? Because it sounds like you're high to me."

"You're the one who's been acting crazy, killing poor Sheraton just because he wanted to have sex with his wife."

I dropped my spoon. I wildly looked around the room, as if finding an exit and running away would somehow save me. Alphonse was silent while he watched me. He enjoyed seeing the panic and stark fear overtake me.

After a few minutes, Alphonse finally spoke. "My only suggestion would have been to do it in a more private place."

"You were there?"

"Unfortunately for you, I don't care for fireworks. I was enjoying a fine Cuban cigar when I heard the commotion. Being a curious fellow, I stepped back into the shadows. I heard and saw everything. Anyone could have come along. It just happened to be me."

"I couldn't pick a different time or place. He was going to rape her."

"He was being romantic with his wife."

"He was attacking her. You would have let him, wouldn't you?"

"No, because I was never there. That will be my official statement. I went home early, alone."

"Official statement my ass! You're going to call the cops on me, right? You're going to be their chief witness, right? You stood by and did nothing. That's a crime too."

"Do you think I'm an idiot? A simple anonymous tip to the police is all that's required in this matter." He mocked me, pantomimed picking up the phone. "Hello? Yes, you know that fellow who's supposedly in

Brazil? If you drag the lake at the Avalon Country Club, I'm sure you'll find proof that he's not in Rio at all. They say golf is a non-violent sport, well, apparently, that's not always true. My wife bludgeoned him to death with a club. Wait…maybe the blunt force trauma to the head didn't kill him but I'm sure he's quite dead now. She weighted him down and threw him into the lake. She was very clever about it. I won't bore you with the details now. When you bring his body to the surface, all will be revealed. Goodbye."

"You bastard."

"Yes, well, at least I've never killed anyone."

"You can't prove it was me."

"I couldn't see very well from my vantage point but I have to ask; did you take the time to wipe all your fingerprints off the club? Are you sure he didn't grab a strand of your hair as you were wrapping him up? Are you positive there's no forensic evidence linking you to him?"

I desperately searched back in my mind for a memory and drew a blank. "I don't know. Anyway, all that time under water, any prints or hair or anything has to be gone now."

"I've been reading up on that. It's amazing what you can learn on the Internet these days. For example, a fingerprint can remain intact under fresh water for quite some time. Now, if you'd thrown poor Sheraton's body into the ocean…that would be a different story. But you didn't. Maybe the print is there. Maybe something else will pop up. Maybe not. Let's have the police take a look, shall we?"

"I can't remember most of it. It's all like a bad dream. You know what happened to me all those years ago."

"Yes, yes, yes, poor little Angie…so sad…defiled when she was so young."

"And I've got the scars to prove it. I was assaulted and almost left for dead. He brutalized me. That's why I had to have Alana by C-section. One psychiatric examination and I have all the proof I need that something so horrible happened to me when I was young that, when I saw it happening again, I went temporarily insane. I'll get off."

Alphonse sighed, finished his glass of wine, and poured another.

"You probably will. Especially if you use Robert as your lawyer. He's the best there is."

"Then why are we having this discussion?"

"Because I know you don't want to go through the terrible publicity of an arrest and a trial. And there's always the slight possibility things might not go your way. Despite the outcome, you'll be ostracized, and the accusation of murder will follow you wherever you go. And what about our daughter? Do you think Alana can stand to go through such a nightmare?"

He was right. Fear cut through me like a knife. "What do you want from me?"

"Ah, finally we come to the point. I have a little favor to ask of you."

"A favor? I'd do you a favor anytime. There's no need for all this drama."

"Okay, it's more of a big favor."

I scooted my chair back and folded my arms. It was negotiation time. "Yes? What sort of favor?"

"Max Burnhardt is casting a movie about the war of the sexes. The lead is perfect for me. I'd finally be doing something of the highest caliber. A guaranteed Academy Award nomination."

"Max hates you."

"I know."

"He'll cast Costner."

"Kevin has a schedule conflict."

"He'd cast anybody but you."

"One of the reasons Max hates me so much is because he's got a hard-on for you. We used to be pretty good friends. Then I married you. He wants you. You know it."

"Yes, he's propositioned me several times…just joking."

"My career is going down the toilet. I'm guest starring this week on some trendy cop show, *Criminal Investigation*. I've got to get back on the big screen. I can play the hell out of this part. And you're going to make sure I get it."

"I'm going to what?"

"Do whatever you have to do. Wine and dine him. Go dancing with him. Go to Palm Springs with him. Fuck his brains out. I know you're an expert at the art of seduction. Wrap him around your little finger, promise him anything, but get him to agree to cast me."

"What if he wants me to divorce you and marry him?"

"Then do it. I won't fight it. I need that part far more than I need you."

"And if I don't?"

"Well, I'll have to tell the police what you did to poor Sheraton. Even if you get off, the scandal will be awful. You won't be able to walk through a grocery story without seeing your face on every newspaper, magazine, and Internet site in the world. Alana's too, probably. Being the daughter of an accused murderess is going to make her quite famous, and not in the good way. I wonder how the kids will treat her at school?"

"All right!" I shouted. "Enough! I get it!"

"So you're going to do it?"

"I have to think about it."

"I'll give you two hours."

"I thought...I mean, I know things have been off between us, but I thought you still loved me."

"I love shiny, gold statues more."

"You're pimping out your own wife."

"Yes, I am."

"You don't have to sound proud about it."

"Before this, I was a broken-down actor who peaked at the age of forty. Forty! Hell, DeNiro and Duvall were just coming into their prime at my age. I was spiraling down and there was no way to stop it. My agent refused to take my calls, it was all but over. Then you had your little adventure and life became full of possibilities again. Proud? Damn, woman, I'm walking on air. And next year, I'll be walking on the red carpet."

He got up and exited the room, leaving me frozen and dead inside. What was I going to do?

LISA

July 6

24

IT WAS LATE. OUR MAID WAS cleaning up the disaster area we call a dining room. Wyatt had started a food fight, and Chase and Liam retaliated with full force. I didn't see how Lupe was going to get the mashed potatoes out of the satin drapes. I went over to her and put a weary hand on her shoulder. "Never mind. I'll order new ones."

"But Mrs. Roth, that will be the third time in six months."

"I don't care. And obviously, Mr. Roth doesn't care. So don't worry. Get what you can off the floor and go to bed. It's been a terrible night."

I was ready to explode. The children had the table manners of animals and used such filthy language that I had told Carson I would never be seen in public with them. Carson wasn't home tonight. Not that they acted much better in front of him, but at least when their father was home, chaos didn't reign quite so supremely.

I went over to the bar and was about to pour myself a huge tumbler of Crystal Head Vodka when my cell phone rang. It was Anjelica. She needed me to come over right away, which was perfect because I needed to get out of this house so I could enjoy my drink in peace. I heard World War Four starting upstairs, and I had no compunctions over leaving the kids unsupervised. I stuck my head in the kitchen and told Lupe that under no circumstances was she to go upstairs. If those fucking kids wanted to set the house on fire, fine by me. As long as Lupe got out okay, I didn't give a damn about the whole place burning to the ground.

I raced over to Anjelica's with my glass of vodka in one hand and the bottle in the other. I got there about the same time as Crystal and Morgan. Morgan laughed, "Were we supposed to bring our own booze?"

Before I could answer, the door opened and Anjelica let us in. I was surprised to see my mother had been called over. I guessed it was comforting for all of the women to see Margaret. Somehow, she seemed like a mother to all of us. Just as we were getting comfortable in the living room, Vivian let herself in, apologizing for being late but she came straight from work the minute she got the call.

We all sighed jealously. To be useful and out in the world. We envied her so much. But this emergency meeting had been called by Anjelica, and we focused on her.

She assured us that Alphonse was out of the house. She promised us we wouldn't be disturbed. Alphonse was down at the club playing gin and smoking cigars. He wouldn't be back for two hours.

I laughed. "At least you know when your husband will be home. I haven't see Carson in three days. One of his clients is a rock star with a penchant for heroin. He's performing the first of six concerts at the Staples Center tonight."

Apparently, this young man named Justin or Jarvis or something like that had to be guarded twenty-four hours a day or he'd score and be shooting up within a matter of hours. Carson liked to personally take care of this addict. Of course, he couldn't always, so a bodyguard was hired. But Carson had stayed close to his client and swore he would not leave his side more than necessary until the concert series in town was complete.

Anjelica assured us it was not a good thing that she knew exactly when Alphonse would be coming home. He had given her two hours to make a decision. She didn't know what to do. By calling us all over here, it meant she was going to be totally honest with her friends, but she needed advice. She loved us more than if we were her sisters. The other women nodded, feeling the same.

I asked why wasn't Dorothy here? Anjelica shook her head. This was a matter of life and death, and as much as she loved Dotty, she didn't fully trust her. Vivian wondered why not. I had a ready answer.

"She doesn't hate her husband."

Mother nodded, "Good thinking."

I surmised, "So I guess this has something to do with hating Alphonse?"

Anjelica took a deep breath, went over to Morgan, and put a loving hand on her shoulder.

"A certain situation has come to light which requires me to share our terrible incident with our dear friends. Is that okay?"

Morgan seemed blindsided, but took Anjelica's hand in hers, "It's your story even more than mine."

Anjelica launched into the whole sordid tale. How she found them… the eight iron…tying him up in the volleyball net…weighing him down…dragging him to the end of the pier and dumping him in the lake. The room was silent even after Anjelica was done. Finally, Mother cleared her throat and spoke up.

"Is Lisa the only one allowed to drink or…"

Anjelica hurried to the bar. "I'm so sorry. Wine?"

Mother chimed in, "I think my daughter has the right idea. After a story like that, we're all going to need something stronger. Preferably single malt."

Anjelica grabbed Lisa's hand and dispensed the vodka while we all continued to absorb Anjelica's astonishing story.

I had finished my drink, so I was lubricated enough to go first. "Well, you could do it. I've met Max—the guy Alphonse wants you to flirt with. He's a little…um…wide…hairy…and he smokes. But other than that, and the fact that Alphonse is the hugest wanker in the world for putting you in this position…"

Mother jumped to her feet, "Lisa, you're joking, right?"

I was adamant, "Mother, I just don't see she has any choice."

Anjelica stared at the carpet, unable to meet her friends' eyes. "I don't. It's not just about me. If Alphonse tells the police what I did, I could get off, or there could be some evidence on his body linking him to me. I know that's not likely, but it's not a chance I'm willing to take. No matter what happens in a courtroom, the tabloids will have a field day with this story and it will ruin Alana, Morgan, and Madelyn. And they've been through hell as it is with the story of Sheraton being gay, leading a double life. Morgan has not been invited to several A-list events since then. God knows what's going to happen to Alana and Maddie at school. It's pretty complicated. I have to do what's right for everyone. I am so beyond furious with Alphonse, I can't even deal with the depth of his depravity. I have one hour and twenty-seven minutes to give him an answer. I know you ladies have never done anything remotely as horrible as I've done. Crystal, Vivian, no matter what you did, the reality is your husbands' actions caused their own death. This is different. I killed in cold blood. And if you can't get past the fact that I've killed someone in such a violent way, I'll understand. You have to believe me when I tell you I was out of my mind. I don't remember most of it. But none of that matters. If Alphonse whispers one word of this, it will be a disaster. That's why I have to do anything and everything he tells me to do."

Vivian got up and went to kneel in front of Anjelica and took her face in her hands. "You're not talking to a room of innocent women."

Morgan said she felt like she was just as guilty for Sheraton's murder as Anjelica was. He was going to rape her. "I don't know what I would have done if Anjelica hadn't come along when she did."

Mother took the center of the room. "You ladies have been smart and powerful. Unfortunately, you married evil men. You've made the world a better place by ridding this planet of those bastards. Anjelica, you need to take a page out of their book. There are more than two options in your situation. You don't have to be your husband's whore, and you don't have to get deported. Has Alphonse got an acting job now?"

"Yes, he's got a pretty good part on a new show, *Criminal Investigation*. He thinks it's slumming."

Mother's eyes sparkled. "Perfect. I'll need to see the script, and then we'll figure out what to do."

Anjelica checked her watch, "Time's almost up. You guys have to go." She whipped around to look out the window in case Alphonse was driving in early. There was no car in the garage, but she asked Vivian where Cassidy was. Vivian was sure her stepdaughter was home. "Why?" she asked.

Angelica shook her head, "Never mind. I just thought I saw her outside the window a second ago. But that would be ridiculous."

Anjelica then started to hyperventilate. "Wait, before you go, we all have to decide how I'm going to do this."

Mother was clearly in charge, "Tell him you'll do it. Call this Max person tonight, right in front of Alphonse. Make plans with Max for two nights from now. That will buy us some time."

Anjelica sighed, "You're talking about killing my husband, aren't you? I've already killed one person. I think I've hit my limit."

We put our arms around each other in a group hug, with Vivian promising, "No. We've got your back on this."

Morgan and I stepped up to the plate: "We'll take care of everything."

Anjelica was sobbing. "I can't believe you love me so much."

Crystal said, "We're bonded for life."

Vivian said, "My life began anew after Hudson died. Crystal is so much happier. Morgan is too. It's going to happen for you, too, Anjelica. We'll make sure of it. I just have to warn you about two things—the nightmares and the terrible guilt that haunts you every day."

Morgan agreed, "Even though Anjelica technically killed my husband, sometimes the guilt overwhelms me. I have these panic attacks. I can't eat, I can't concentrate, I'm living on Chardonnay and Xanax."

Crystal and Anjelica nodded. The men they killed were in hell for sure. But that didn't mean they didn't suffer terrible remorse for the murders they'd committed.

Anjelica put her head in her hands. "If I had to do it again, of course, I would. But I'm not a killer by nature. I don't have it in me...or at least I didn't. At first, I felt release from the bondage of the past. But then, the reality of what I had done set in. Sometimes I think Sheraton's ghost is following me around. I'll see his reflection in a shop window or the rearview mirror of my car. It's unnerving. Quite frightful, actually. I suppose the trauma will go away in time, but if we're going to go through with this plan for Alphonse, girls, you have to know there's a terrible cost to pay, peace of mind."

Vivian seemed more settled. "The nightmares, the guilt, the remorse. They lessen in time. And it's not like we weren't living lives of constant tension even when our husbands were alive."

Crystal trembled, "I believe you, Vivian, but I'm afraid to go to sleep at night. And even if I do manage to fall asleep, I'll wake up in the middle of the night and Jonathan will be there, sitting on the edge of our bed, telling me how I'm a disgusting, mutilated whore, yet a slut at the same time for wanting to move on with my life with another man. And how dare I, after killing him. He says he knows he was no saint, but he never murdered anyone. I killed him and afterward I was glad. But taking someone's life...even someone as horrible as Jonathan...it begins to torture you. I'm always afraid he will reach from beyond the grave and haunt me the rest of my life. I don't think it's a nightmare. He's haunting me."

Mother sat with Crystal and promised she was not being haunted by her husband's dead ghost. It was all a dream. She also promised she'd give Crystal a hell of a pill that would knock her right out at night and keep her out till morning. As for the nightmares, that was just their subconscious minds working through the mental anguish they'd suffered. The nightmares would go away, she promised, followed by sweet dreams.

Morgan filled up everyone's glasses again, lifted her glass high in a toast, and said she'd take whatever mental torture came her way. If we're really going to do this with Alphonse, let's do it. "Here's to ridding the world of another bag of scum."

Ten minutes later, Alphonse came in and there wasn't a sign that anyone had been there. Lisa's vodka was gone and all the glasses had been cleaned and put up on their shelves over the wet bar. Alphonse was acting especially smug.

"Well, did you make up your mind?"

"Yes. You win. I'll call Max now."

As Angelica dialed the phone, it was so hard for her to keep the smallest hint of a smile from the corners of her face.

ZAC

July 6

25

OF COURSE, I DIDN'T KNOW WHAT was going on. I was walking down the middle of the street while the Lake Ladies' cabal broke up. I was just kicking a beer can into the storm drain, on my way home, smoking a cigarette, which was verboten in my house, when Cassidy ran smack into me. She screamed and punched me. I gently held her. "Cass, it's me. You okay?"

Cassidy calmed down enough to focus and realize what was going on. "Oh, Zac. Yes, I'm okay. I just wasn't watching where I was going."

"And you were running about ninety miles an hour. Where were you going?"

"Home."

"From where?"

"I dunno. Alana's."

"Don't make me interrogate you. Talk to me. It's alright. Look at you, you're shaking all over. Come here."

I wrapped her in my arms. There we stood in the middle of the street, swaying back and forth. I was not about to let her go until her breathing slowed. But we heard voices coming from the Louis' house. Cassidy pushed out of my embrace.

"We have to go."

She dragged me into the bushes where we waited until all the women were gone.

"Seems like you weren't the only one at Alana's house. That was practically the whole clique, wasn't it?" I pointed out.

"Um…Yeah, they had company. I was company too—sort of."

I held her tightly and tilted her chin so that she had to look directly into my eyes. "What did I do to deserve this?"

"This?"

"Distrust."

"I don't distrust you."

"Then why are you holding back from me?"

"I was at Alana's house."

"So you've graduated to becoming one of the Ladies of the Lake?"

"Don't be silly."

"Then why were you there?"

"To see Alana, of course."

"Ah, that's the lie. Don't you think I know you, Cassidy Elaine Montgomery? I know every expression you have, every mood you feel, every thought you think…at least I did until now. Now you're closed off to me. Why? Something's going on. Why won't you tell me?"

"It's not because I don't trust you, because of course I do. It's just… I've found myself in the middle of something. It's not my secret I'm keeping. Please believe me."

"I don't know what to believe."

"How about, I love you."

I wasn't ready for that. I stepped away and stared at her intently. I was trying to read her mind and her soul.

She declared it again, "I love you. Do you at least believe that?"

I said nothing.

Cassidy was devastated. "I guess not."

Before she could turn away, I reached out for her and drew her into a kiss. It was one of those first kisses that had been building up inside two people for so long that, by the time it finally happened, it seemed to go on and on forever.

Finally we broke apart to breathe and for me to say, "Yes."

The next kiss involved some movements of hands and repositioning of some clothes. We finally came to our senses and stopped.

I laughed, "Oh, in case you couldn't tell, I love you too."

Cassidy pulled my arm, "Let's go to my place."

We got in the house just as Vivian was returning from Anjelica's. We raced up the stairs and quietly shut the door to Cassidy's bedroom. Vivian called out from downstairs, "Cass?"

Cassidy opened her door, "Yeah, Viv?"

"Have you been home all night?"

"Yeah, why?"

"Oh one of my friends thought she saw you roaming about."

"Not me. Goodnight." She shut the door. When she turned, my look of love had hardened to one of confusion.

"Well, at least I know I'm not the only one you're lying to."

"I told you, it's not my lie to tell or keep."

"But it was you over at Alana's house. And don't tell me you were with Alana. I happen to know she and James are at a Maroon 5 concert tonight."

"Okay, here's what I can tell you. I was there but not really."

"Why are you dicking around with me?"

"I'm not. I was outside the house."

"Trimming the trees?"

"Spying."

"Why? Does this have something to do with Clara?"

"That's what I can't tell you."

"Then how can you say you love me?"

"Because I'm protecting you by not telling you. It has something to do with my father's death and all the other strange things that have been going on here. It will all come to light soon enough with the cops, I think."

"Cass, you're talking about death and cops, and you're clearly in over your head."

"Yes, but I won't be for long. By this time tomorrow, I'll have given all my information to someone else. Someone who will know how to best use it, and then I'll be out of it. We're going up to Oregon soon anyway. Let's just go off to college. This is a sick and twisted place, and I can't wait to get away. No matter what truths may come out, we'll be far away where people don't care what we've been through this summer. Please?"

"Damn. Cass, you know how hard it is for me to trust anyone. Seven foster homes in six years. Dorothy can feed me all the homemade soup she wants, but it can't undo the damage of being abandoned over and over again."

"I know. That was a sweet little speech you gave me outside…about how well you know me. Well, right back at ya. We've been in love for a long time, we could just never say the words because our childhoods were so fucked up. This community, these people we call our parents… they're all batshit crazy. The power and the money and the publicity… it all got to them. We've got to make our escape."

"Yeah, I agree, but I only have enough money for the first year. If I don't get a job, I can't stay in school, and the idea of being left behind by you is unthinkable. And forget about you paying my way. I know you're coming into a lot of money in a couple of months. But that's your money."

Cassidy started laughing.

"Don't you think I know about your damn pride? I wouldn't offer you a goddamn cent. You are going to make it in this world without any financial help from me. But I'll be with you, in every other way."

I was so sucked into the vortex of Cassidy's emotions that we fell back onto the bed and began undressing each other. Cassidy stopped. "Maybe we shouldn't."

I smiled, "It's okay, I've been keeping this in my pocket for a year just for you…for a moment just like this…for a moment I knew was inevitable."

We giggled as I pulled one condom out of my wallet, and then suddenly, we weren't laughing anymore. We wanted to be a part of each other. We needed each other more than we needed anything. This was not teenage exploration or experimentation. This was the beginning of a life-long love affair. And when two soulmates spend a life together, it's always right and good, even through bad times. But the beginning is the sweetest of all…

26

I WOKE TO THE MUFFLED SOUND of Cassidy talking on her cell phone in the bathroom. I got up, slipped into my boxers, and silently moved to the closed door. I could kind of hear Cassidy's end of the conversation because the tile in the bathroom made any sound bounce around.

"Clara, I can't talk now. My boyfriend is asleep in the other room. He's going to wake up any minute. I've told you everything I know. I wouldn't have even been aware of my stepmom's secret meeting last night if she hadn't called all her girlfriends about it and the tap you gave me to put on her cell picked it up."

I stuck my fist in my mouth to keep from gasping. Cassidy and Clara had tapped Vivian's phone? I hadn't thought it would go this far. What the fuck was going on here?

"Clara, I'm done. No more spying or lying. I'm keeping all this from someone I really love, and I won't let it ruin what could be the best thing in my life."

There was silence. Then, "Yes, all the women are responsible for what's been going on with the terrible events at Avalon. I even heard Viv's name mentioned in connection with Dad's death when I was eavesdropping at the window. But I can't confront her about it. We don't have enough proof. And frankly, while I don't love Vivian, you're not my favorite person either. You were going to break up my family. Well, my stepmom beat you to it. Dad did a lot of shitty things and he paid the price. I love him but no longer admire him or want to see his death avenged. He brought it all on himself. Vivian's running Dad's company and doing a damn good job of it. You want her to go to jail, you make it happen. I'm out."

I heard Cassidy end the conversation and ran back and jumped into the bed. Cassidy came out of her gleaming white bathroom. Everything in the bathroom was white. The tile, the cupboards, the shower door, the toilet, even the mirror had a white frame. In contrast to that, her queen-sized bed was black. Her bedroom carpet was black. The walls were white, but all the furniture was black. That was Cassidy. Everything was either black or white, and now I understood why she was so upset. She was living in a grey area now. Something had happened and she couldn't metaphorically file it in the white drawer or in the black drawer.

She jumped onto the bed and slipped into my arms, telling me that last night was the best thing that ever happened to her.

I meant it when I said, "Me too."

We laid there for a while in silence, then I got up and started to get dressed. Cassidy pouted a bit. She knew her stepmom had already gone to work, and she had had plans to dazzle me with her kitchen skills by whipping up some scrambled eggs.

"I'd love to stay but I promised my mom I'd do my laundry."

Cassidy giggled, "That's one of the reasons I love you so much. You live in the real world. You're the only one of us who does their own laundry. Hey, when we get to college, will you teach me?"

"Sure." I kissed her goodbye, but that kiss turned into another and another, and it was about fifteen minutes before I got out of there. I reminded myself to go buy some more condoms.

While Cassidy thought I was doing my laundry, I was really driving towards the police station. Now both of us had lied to each other. Not the best way to start a serious relationship.

27

I WALKED THROUGH A MAZE OF desks looking for Detective Daniels. I found him in the back of the room shouting into the phone, "Search warrant? We had probable cause. What do you mean it's inadmissible, the guy's as guilty as hell." There were about three seconds of silence, then Daniels shouted even louder, "Go fuck yourself." He slammed down his phone.

A guy at the desk next to him whose nameplate read "Det. Rameriz" said, "I told you."

Just then a man in a light-colored suit and a head that did not have a hair on it came up, "Tone it down, Shaun."

Detective Daniels apologized but was still furious. "Sorry, Captain. It's just these fucking judges. They don't get it. Dillion should be looking at life in jail. Now he's not even going to see the inside of a courtroom."

The captain patronizingly patted Daniels' head. "I know. You did your best on this case. We'll get him next time."

"I doubt it."

The captain moved off, and Rameriz asked Daniels, "What happened to that guy we nicknamed 'Boy Scout'? Two years ago, when you moved up to this desk, you were all gung ho, wanting to catch all the bad guys and save the goddamn planet. Now you're just backing off on a suspect because the captain told you to?"

"Yeah, well, two years has taught me a lot. This world is past saving. Fuck 'em. Fuck 'em all."

Just then, he looked up and noticed me. "What the hell do you want?"

"Well, I was hoping you'd instill in me a love for all mankind, but I guess I came on the wrong day."

Rameriz cracked up.

Daniels motioned for me to take a seat next to his desk, which I probably should mention was as orderly and tidy as I've ever seen anyone's desk before. Maybe the guy had O.C.D. or something.

"Okay, wiseass…Zac, right?"

"That's right."

"What are you doing here?"

"Well, over at Avalon, we haven't heard much from you since you barged into my parents' house and treated them like murder suspects."

"Nonsense. I was all milk and honey."

"Whatever. Anyway. Since there's been these deaths and disappearances and stuff, I was wondering if you had a lead on any of them."

"You rich kids think the world revolves around you. Well it's a big, nasty city out there and real people are committing real crimes. You wealthy sons-of-bitches want to run off with your boyfriend or fuck yourselves to death or have a bad encounter with a garage door, be my guest."

"Okay. I was just wondering. You don't have to yell."

"Sorry. Bad day."

"Well, I'll make it better by leaving." And I walked out thinking if something was mucked up with the country club gang, Cassidy knew more about it than the police.

LISA

July 17

28

MORGAN AND I WALKED NONCHALANTLY ONTO the police office set of *Criminal Investigation*. I only saw Alphonse, and that was way across the soundstage. We had bought wigs and did our makeup to look like it was camera-ready. We blended in with all the other extras.

We got to work quickly. We knew what to do. Morgan assessed the set and identified who was who—the director, lighting guys, sound guys, hair and makeup and, most importantly, the prop master. He was standing in front of a long table of props, handcuffs, a fake knife, a cell phone. Morgan quickly spotted the item she was interested in—the gun.

She turned and looked at me, and I knew that was the signal. I went over to the prop master named Doug, a balding, paunchy man with a nervous twitch. I poured on the charm, pretending to be just one of the actors. I knew there was no way he could identify me later. When

I'd looked in the mirror earlier, I didn't recognize myself. I acted like a vapid siren as I pretended to flirt with him, "mistaking" him for one of the actors. A voice came over the PA system: Alphonse's gun scene was just about to be shot. I gave the slightest of nods to Morgan and she reached in her purse, made sure no one was looking, and switched the prop gun with the gun she'd had in her handbag. She was wearing gloves, and the guns matched perfectly. Thanks to some recon Anjelica had done earlier, we knew exactly what kind of pistol would be used.

I then broke off my conversation with Doug, and Morgan and I slipped out a side door not many of the crew knew about. Anjelica had alerted us to the perfect getaway path. All in all, the whole thing took about ten minutes.

We rushed over to Anjelica's house sans disguises. Alana was in the living room watching a movie her dad made about five or six years ago. She greeted us. "Mom's upstairs. She'll be down in a minute. Look at my dad. He's so handsome. Too bad the TV show he's shooting today is lame."

Anjelica came downstairs dressed to the nines. Alana was a bit surprised. "You and Dad going out somewhere?"

"No I'm having dinner with an old friend named Max."

"Why are you doing that?"

"What, I can't have a social life apart from your dad? Max is a dear friend whom I haven't seen in ages, and we just want to catch up."

"Whatever."

Anjelica turned to us. "Morgan! Lisa! How nice of you to drop by. I can't chat long but I have time for a glass of wine. Alana, would you go upstairs and get my emerald earrings? I think they would go perfectly with this dress." Alana was reluctant to do anyone a favor of any kind but she condescended to obey her mom.

Crystal and Margaret came in the front door. All eyes were on me and Morgan. Anjelica asked, "Lisa, did you do it?"

I answered confidently, "Just as planned."

"And no one saw Morgan make the switch."

I nodded, "I kept the prop master busy, but I have eyes in the back of my head. We're clear."

Anjelica asked, "Where's the script?"

Morgan handed it to her.

Margaret told her, "Throw it in the fire."

It just so happened it was a cool evening, and Anjelica had a roaring fire going at the time. Morgan tossed in the script and it started to burn just as Alana came down.

"Here, Mom."

"Thank you, Darling. You know, I'm suddenly not feeling very well. I don't think I'll go out tonight after all." She pulled out her cell and dialed. "Max? It's Anjelica, Darling. I know, I was just getting ready to leave the house when I started feeling a bit faint. I may have a touch of the flu. It's been going around. I'm afraid I'll have to cancel. So sorry. Talk to you soon, Luv. Ciao." She hung up.

Alana was confused, "You don't have the flu. What did you blow him off for? What was all that about wanting to catch up with such a dear old friend crap?"

"What can I say, Alana. I changed my mind. Now why don't you go to the movies or something. I'm going to change into a robe and slippers and just rest and visit with my friends."

"Mom, you are losing it. But whatever. Bye." She grabbed her coat and left.

Anjelica asked Morgan, "When should I hear something?"

I answered, "Any minute now. It was the last scene of the day."

Sure enough, Anjelica's phone rang about ten minutes later. We gripped our wine glasses as Anjelica held the phone slightly away from her ear so we could hear the producer, Calvin Smith, on the other end. He was trying to keep his voice calm, but you could tell he was about to fall to pieces.

"Angie, I don't know how to tell you this. There's been an accident. I don't know how it happened. I mean, I know but…Let me start over. Alphonse was guest starring on our show, playing this bad guy who was on his way to be locked up for life, but instead, his character was supposed to grab a gun out of one of the guard's holsters and put the gun to his head. Then he has this whole speech about how he'd rather die than be locked up. And Alphonse did all that. He was great. I mean, really great. But then it came time for him…I mean, for his character to put the gun to his head and pull the trigger. So that's what Al did. And…aw, fuck, Angie, there's no good way to say this. There were supposed to be blanks in the gun. Alphonse's a pro at firearms. The prop master checked it twice before we did the scene. I don't know how it happened. It was a real bullet. I have no idea how it got in there, but it went right into his brain and killed him instantly. Of course, we called the paramedics, but there was nothing they could do. He was pronounced dead on the scene. Oh, Christ, I'm so sorry. I mean, this kind of thing has happened before. It's not unheard of. But I just don't understand how it happened here. We do stunts like this all the time. Nothing's ever gone wrong. Goddamit, I'm so sorry, Angie."

We all looked at each other, then real tears started to flow from Anjelica's face. "I can't believe it. It's just too terrible. Do I need to go somewhere? The police station? The morgue? Should I see him?"

"No, no point in that. The authorities will be in touch with you later. I'm so sorry, baby."

Anjelica was gulping sobs, "I just can't talk, I have to go." She hung up and knelt on the floor. "I loved him so much. And Alana adores him. She'll be devastated. But he was going to have me arrested for murder. What choice did I have?"

Margaret reached down, grabbed Anjelica's hand, and pulled her to her feet. "Stop crying. Alphonse is not worthy of those tears. And Alana's broken heart will heal. It was horrible. It was ugly. But it's done. You have the capability of being stronger than you have ever been. Tap down deep inside yourself. Find that strength."

Anjelica stopped crying. She went to the green velvet sofa and sat between Morgan and myself. She thanked us both again.

I said, "Don't thank me. I was just Morgan's wingman on this."

Morgan squeezed her hand, "Anjelica, you risked everything to save me. There's nothing I wouldn't do for you."

I was thinking it through. "This is the first one that's really going to look suspicious to the cops. That Detective Daniels has been sniffing around."

Anjelica piped up, "I think we can handle him. And when I say 'we,' I mean Crystal."

Crystal shook her head. "I actually like this guy and he genuinely likes me. I know we met under odd circumstances, but I thought I might really go out with him. I think there's something there. He's so good. He's the polar opposite of Jonathan. He treats me like a porcelain doll. I could use some kindness from a man for a change. I don't want to risk all that by losing him."

Margaret's response was quick and decisive. "Marry the man for all I care. But Lisa is right. We can't brush this over. The police will do a full-on investigation. He'll have no way to connect you, Morgan, or you, Lisa, to what happened to Alphonse. You're friends with his wife but that's all. Crystal, this is going to raise red flags everywhere. You have to handle Detective Daniels, and through him, the cops. Screw his brains out if you want, but keep an eye on him. Monitor the investigation as best you can without arousing suspicion. If he starts to get a whiff of the truth, tell us. We'll be out of the country within two hours. Can you do that for us?"

Crystal teared up a little but her voice was clear and strong as she said, "I can do anything for you, my friends."

CRYSTAL

July 17

29

A FEW HOURS LATER, I WAS back at home, staring for an hour at the business card Shaun had given me. I knew what I had to do but I hated it. I checked the clock. It was only 8:30. Not too late to call. Finally, sick of the war going on in my head, I just picked up the phone and dialed. Damnit. He answered. I'd been hoping to get voice mail.

The mariachi band was a little loud, but other than that, the Mexican restaurant was delightful. It was on a street called Olvera. I told Shaun I'd never been there before. He threw his head back and laughed. I couldn't tell if he was laughing at me or if somehow I'd said something funny. He assured me that he was most definitely laughing at me. He bet me ten bucks that I'd never gone outside the borders of Beverly

Hills, except maybe the occasional trip to Malibu.

I assured him I had grown up in a middle-class family in Sylmar. I graduated from high school, and I got a job in West Hollywood as a waitress in a swank restaurant. I commuted all the way from Sylmar.

I bit into a chip and then went on, "I know I didn't get the job because I'm smart or efficient. I got it because of…well…my looks. We lived in a trailer. Yep, I'm trailer trash. I don't know who my father was. My mom was what they would now call a 'cougar.' She got older, but the men she brought home didn't. And they always needed something from her—money to fix their Harleys, money to bail them out of jail, money for drugs. She didn't work, but she did collect welfare, so she lured these men with the promise of money for whatever they wanted… money that didn't go to lunch for me or clothes. I always joke I have a father complex but I guess it's true. Mother issues to boot. No one ever took care of me. I was left to fend for myself. Then one day, Jonathan walked into the restaurant and into my life and offered me all the things I'd never had before. Security…love…someone to take care of me. He was an answer to a prayer. I was so stupid. I was so crazy in love with him that I never stopped to ask myself what he saw in me. He wanted a trophy wife, that's all. He never loved me. He never loved anyone but himself. But he showered me with so much stuff that I mistook his spending for love. And why wouldn't I? I'd never had money before. At first, I loved the money as much as I loved Jonathan. That much money is dazzling. I became friends with Anjelica, Vivian, Morgan, Lisa, and to some extent, Dotty. They taught me all about labels and designers, and it wasn't long before I was sure I was better than all the friends I'd left behind in Sylmar.

"It didn't occur to me that I hadn't earned that money. I spent like an addict. I loved the way I looked, I loved the way the saleswomen treated me, I loved being Jonathan's trophy. But then, Jonathan withdrew. His real personality came to light. He didn't treat me like a princess any more. Every once in a while he'd call me 'white trash' just to remind me of my roots. He enjoyed hurting me…controlling me. And as the days went on, I started to feel like that lost, lonely little girl again. But I'm not a little girl. I'm a grown-up. And I'm starting to take responsibility for my own happiness. For better or worse, that's sort of where I am right now. I'm sorry. I seem to have diarrhea of the mouth. I'm hogging the conversation."

Shaun leaned in, "No. Keep going. Please. What happened? What changed?"

"One day, I was standing in the middle of the cosmetics department in Bloomingdale's and an overwhelming sense of sadness came over me. I looked around at all the women. And they all looked like robots to me. I was a robot too. I was going to spend my life going from store to store, never contributing anything to society, never creating anything of beauty or value. It was like there was a hole in the ground and I was sinking. A horrible depression came over me. Jonathan thought a good shrink and some meds would fix me right up. I threw myself into charity work. The girls and I hosted party after party, raising money for every cause conceivable. But I knew the only thing that would make me happy. A baby. Jonathan wanted a son and so did I, and I was determined to have one. But all the determination in the world didn't make me pregnant. I saw doctors, went through procedures, only to feel like a failure every month."

I hadn't meant to go on like that, and I certainly hadn't meant to cry. I don't know why I opened up like that. I must have made Shaun horribly uncomfortable.

"Shaun, I'm so sorry. This is terrible first date conversation. But at least now you know I'm no prize. I wasn't shocked when Jonathan started cheating on me. I think he started sleeping around the day after our wedding. And I put up with it. Well, that's it. That's my story. I know we haven't ordered yet but maybe we should ask for the check. If I were you, I'd want to get out of here and away from me as soon as possible."

"Crystal, don't you know how special you are? I've never met anyone like you. I admit I was struck by lightning the first time I saw you. But your face and your body are not the most beautiful parts of you. You're tender and kind and generous, and hell...I could go through a million words to describe you. All those things you said about yourself only made me think more of you. I'm sorry that you can't have a baby because you'd be the most wonderful mom in the world. But if you had a child with that asshole Jonathan, that wouldn't have been ideal."

"Ideal is off the table for me. And if you knew some of the things I've done…"

"None of that matters. And you deserve an ideal life more than you know. It all depends on your definition of ideal."

"What's yours?"

"Finding the right woman. Preferably blonde, petite, with a beautiful smile and grey/blue eyes. Then I'd marry her and, if she happened to be the kind of woman who couldn't get pregnant, we'd travel around the world looking for a baby who didn't have any parents, just waiting for us to come along. And the three of us would be a happy little family. Ideal."

Tears stung my eyes. My heart was beating so hard I thought I would pass out. "Most men wouldn't feel that way."

"I'm not most men."

"This conversation is getting too serious. If you really knew me, you wouldn't like what you learned."

"You just spent the past fifteen minutes telling me all I need to know. You went on so long, the waiter over there has made three attempts to come over to our table to take our order, but he could see he'd be interrupting."

"Sorry. But for you to say all those things to me about the future, you'd have to have made up your mind about me very fast. Too fast."

"Neither of us are spring chickens. We've been around the block a few times. So it doesn't take me long to recognize a gem when I see one."

"You're talking about maybe…someday…"

"Falling in love with you? Crystal, I have a feeling every man you've ever met has fallen in love with you."

"You really are a piece of work, mister. You could charm the hell out of anyone. And under any other circumstances, I'd be so happy with you right now. But…things are so complicated…"

"Relax. This is a first date. Just keep an open mind. Let's say, hypothetically, it's six months down the line and I've convinced you that you can't live without me. Then there's no reason we can't be happy.

Well, there would be one reason."

My brain was bouncing around inside my head. I felt drunk. I thought of all the things my friends and I had done, how I was supposed to be there keeping an eye on Shaun and instead, I was living a fairy tale. I couldn't imagine ever feeling redeemed for what I did to Jonathan.

"Shaun. I can't talk about the future, hypothetically or not. But I am curious. What would that one thing be that would keep us from being happy?"

"Jonathan's money. I'd insist you give it all away and we live on my meager cop's salary."

I felt my smile grow until I was grinning like a fool. And all I could say was, "Sounds ideal."

Just as we ordered our margaritas, Shaun's phone rang. He apologized but warned me that it happened a lot, that it came with the territory. He answered his phone, listened for a second, then his handsome face twisted into a look of anger that I'd never seen before.

"Two hours ago? Why didn't anyone tell me?" Silence again. And then, "What do you mean I haven't been taking all this seriously. There's been nothing to take seriously until now." He listened a second longer before exploding, "You're putting Hollister on the case? No fuckin' way. He's a moron. I'm staying on this case." He paused again, "Okay, Hollister can do all the digging he wants, but I'm still involved." He hung up.

I knew what had just happened. I stirred my margarita and focused on the lime floating in my glass. I couldn't look him in the eyes.

Shaun put his cell back in his coat pocket and finished off his drink in one long gulp. I waited. The silence spoke volumes.

Finally, Shaun spoke. "Aren't you going to ask me what that was about?"

I stalled. "I don't know what cops are allowed to talk about and what's classified. I thought I shouldn't be nosy."

I couldn't tell from the tone of his voice if he believed me or not. "Well, this is certainly not classified. It's on the Internet already and going to splashed all over the news tomorrow."

I tried to sound curious. "What happened?"

"Your little elite group of friends' run of bad luck continues. Alphonse Louis just had a little accident on the TV set where he was working."

I was so terrified, I think the guilt on my face could have easily been interpreted as shock. "An accident? Is he okay?"

"Well, his brains are splattered all over the wall of the set, so I'm gonna guess no, he's not okay."

"What are you talking about?"

"He was in character when he put a gun to his head that was supposed to be loaded with blanks. But they weren't blanks. They were real bullets. It had been loaded with blanks by the prop master himself, checked several times. No one seems to know how those bullets got in there."

"It seems impossible. How violent and terrible. That's unheard of."

"Not exactly. Accidents like that have happened before. A young actor in the 80's had that exact thing happen to him. And Bruce Lee's son was killed on a movie set in a similar way."

I started fishing, "You keep calling it an accident. But doesn't it seem someone did it on purpose?"

"Hell yeah. And it's a damn coincidence that four best golfing buddies die boom, boom, boom, boom. And I don't believe in coincidences. There's nothing to connect these incidents except the fact that these guys were friends. The first three are easily understood, but this one we'll have to treat like a murder investigation. And we'll have to reopen all the other Avalon Estates cases too."

We'd expected this but it still froze my heart to hear it. I had to tell the girls right away.

"Don't worry about me. Seems like you need to go, get over to that crime scene, and do your job." Then, I hated myself for what I said next because I had to go into spy mode, "Then call me when you're done. Okay? I don't care how late it is."

Shaun seemed surprised but pleased. "You sure?"

"I'm very sure."

30

ALL THE LADIES ASSEMBLED IN MY living room the next morning. All except Dotty. We just couldn't include her in anything anymore. With Alphonse's death, we'd crossed a line. There was no going back, and secrecy was of the utmost importance.

The coffee and bagels I had put out for everyone lay untouched on the coffee table. The dark circles under everyone's eyes were a telltale sign that no one had slept the night before. I had just finished updating them on my date with Shaun.

Lisa asked, "And did he call you last night?"

I paced as I talked. I was so wired. I hadn't slept a wink either. "Yes, he called me about two in the morning. He told me they dusted for prints. Now they're having the computer go through everyone who worked on the set to see if they come up with a match."

Morgan grimaced. "Which they won't. They won't find any prints except maybe the prop master's and Alphonse's. And who's going to notice two unaccounted-for extras who were there for ten minutes. I was surprised how loose security was. I thought it would be much more difficult."

I continued, "Then Shaun told me they're going to question everyone on the set that day, ask them for alibis, ask them if they saw anyone or anything unusual that day. Since none of the cast or crew is guilty, they'll draw another big blank."

Morgan grabbed Lisa's hand. "Unless we were spotted. I know we were careful and our plan went like clockwork—still, if someone did see one of us, I'm going to take all the blame, Lisa. You were just a lookout. I did the actual gun switch."

That made me think of something else. "They still think someone switched out the blanks for real bullets. They don't know yet that a duplicate gun was switched with the prop. They will figure that out eventually, though."

Anjelica said, "That's okay. It won't lead them anywhere. I can't thank you two enough for doing this for me."

I had to caution all of them. "We're not out of the woods. They're reopening all the cases. I don't see how they can connect me to Jonathan's death, or you, Vivian, to Hudson's death. And since Morgan and I are not related except by friendship to Alphonse, and Anjelica's connection to Sheraton is even weaker, the cops will have an impossible job of putting it all together. I hope. We've drawn attention to ourselves because we're all part of Avalon. We have to be extra careful."

Anjelica was cocky. "Let them investigate. Alphonse made me nervous about the possibility of leaving a fingerprint on the club I used to knock out Sheraton, but I'm sure I was careful. I was on autopilot when I got rid of the body...I mean, I was truly nuts. A temporary insanity plea wouldn't be a strategy; it would be the truth. But it won't come to that. Now that my blackmailing husband is gone, no one can trace me to Sheraton's death."

Lisa channeled her mother for a moment, "Still, it's important to stay one step ahead of the cops. That's why you've got to keep seeing Detective Daniels, Crystal."

I sank to the floor, "I know. But I like this guy so much. I feel so guilty for spying on him."

Lisa leaned down and patted me on the back, "When all this is over, you can take a nice trip to Hawaii. Right now, you have to stay focused."

I loved these women so much. And they weren't asking me to do anything but keep my head on straight and be smart. "I will. But I keep thinking about the old days. Barbeques and parties and late night swims. Our beautiful lake…the boys playing golf…the kids, when they were young, on the swings. We were so happy. So normal. How did it come to this?"

The room was silent for a moment before Morgan softly said, "They pushed, and pushed and pushed…until we had no choice but to push back."

VIVIAN

July 20

31

ALPHONSE WOULD HAVE LOVED HIS FUNERAL. Being a B+ actor, he had enough friends and fans to fill the chapel to overflowing. Many fans sat outside on the lawn. Big screen TVs and speakers had been set up in anticipation of the event.

There's nothing actors love more than to talk about how much they love each other. In some cases, it seemed a little hypocritical since several of the men had been in serious competition with Alphonse for parts for many years. Yet on and on they went, loving the sound of their own voices as they lauded someone who could only honestly be called a mediocre talent. Of course, that's not what we heard from the pulpit that day. From listening to some of the eulogies, you would have thought Laurence Olivier had died. Actors also love to cry, so the hankies were out and the tears flowed freely. I looked over at Anjelica.

Her tears were real. She had been with Alphonse so long. They had been a good couple for much of their marriage. But life in the spotlight had turned Alphonse into a cold, mean-spirited man who was willing to ruin his wife's life, all over one movie role.

It was strange to look around and not see Hudson, Sheraton, or Jonathan. While the focus of the service was Alphonse's career (complete with clips from some of his better parts), anyone who really knew Alphonse could no longer think of this death without thinking about the other three friends of his being taken suddenly out of their lives. The most suspicious of all being Detective Daniels, who was sitting next to Crystal with a skeptical look on his face.

All us girls played our parts to the hilt—having had lots of practice by now of looking bereaved and consoling the widow. But Alana's pain was no act. The look of agony on her face broke my heart. It was the same look Cassidy had after her father died. She still has it occasionally. I try to fill the gaps, be the best stepmom I can be, but work has taken over my life; and every day, Hudson becomes more and more a memory.

Alana clung to her mother, and had her friends right behind her, literally and metaphorically. Zac held Cassidy's hand. It was clear that the grief Cassidy, James, and Madelyn had for their own fathers was mixed together with grief for Alana and her loss.

When all the over-acting was done, Alana surprised her mother by getting up to say a few words.

"I don't know what's happening to all of us. It's like a bad dream. I felt so bad for Cassidy, James, and Madelyn when their fathers were suddenly torn out of their lives. But now, I really know how they feel. I mean, I know James and Madelyn's dad is still alive but he left them, and that's painful too. I just never knew anything could hurt this bad. I just wanted to say to all of you that I loved my dad very much. But some of you haven't spoken the whole truth about him. He wasn't always a good person."

Worried, I looked over to see how Daniels was reacting. Alana certainly had his attention.

Alana went on. "Dad was just a person like everybody else. He had his good days and his bad days. Sometimes it was hard to live with him. I don't mean to disrespect him. I loved him, and I know he loved me. But I want us to be sad that a man died who had faults, just like we all do. Let's not pretend he didn't. Let's miss the man he really was instead of a made-up version of him. That's all I have to say."

When she sat down, her mom hugged her tightly. I leaned over and said, "That was very wise and wonderful, Darling."

Alana took my hand for a moment, "Thank you, Vivian."

All I remember about the next part of the day was being stuck in a mad crush of people. We didn't think we would be missed, so we skipped the reception that was thrown by the studio. Anjelica just stayed a few moments to receive gratuitous hugs from the more important people, and then she slipped away to join us at my house for our own version of Alphonse's wake.

Once we got to the house, we assessed the situation. As usual, the kids disappeared. We sent Crystal off to keep an eye on Daniels, pick his brain, find out what he thought, what kind of math he was doing.

Sometime later, Crystal called us from a bar where they were having drinks. She had excused herself to go to the ladies room to give us an update. The investigation was ongoing, but they had no leads and no suspects. The entire cast and crew had been questioned, and the cops were frustrated because they were coming up empty. Crystal had a feeling there was something Shaun wasn't telling her: he was a little distant—not cold, but reserved. She wasn't going to push for any more information. This was a tricky situation. She hung up, and we started drinking and pacing. Four friends gone. No policeman worth half a badge would consider it a coincidence...unless they believed in the supernatural and considered perhaps that someone had put a curse on the men of Avalon Estates.

Margaret's presence calmed us down. She reminded us there was nothing to do now but keep a low profile and wait for the cops to do their thing. Without a shred of evidence, they could speculate all they wanted but in the end, they would come up empty. The hard part was over. We just had to keep their wits about them and all would be well.

She looked over at Lisa. "Except for you, my sweet daughter. I wish with all my heart we could help you rid yourself of that horrible husband of yours. But that would be just one too many."

Lisa assured us that was okay. She had new hope that she and Carson could become close again.

"Carson didn't show up today. Where's his loyalty?" Morgan observed.

Lisa explained that he was still babysitting his heroin-addicted rock star client. He'd been away for days, but she expected him home tonight.

Then I realized, "Dotty and Tommy didn't show either. In the mad crush, I didn't notice it at the time. I wonder if Dotty had felt the freeze-out from the group once we kicked her out of the loop?"

Morgan was sorry if that was true and her feelings were hurt, but she didn't understand why Tommy wasn't there.

Anjelica agreed. She knew that Alphonse, like all the other club buddies, had a soft spot in his heart for Tommy, had lent him a lot of money over the years, never expecting or asking to get it back.

Margaret suggested they not worry about that now. It was getting late. They should disperse. Lisa asked her mom if she wanted to come over for dinner.

Margaret asked if the kids were there.

Lisa stuck her tongue out and said, "Yes, Lupe was watching them now." Margaret then asked if Carson was really coming home later in the night. Lisa nodded again.

Margaret got to her feet relatively quickly. "That's two reasons to decline your invitation."

Everyone left, and I suddenly felt the need to check on Cassidy. I pulled out my phone from my purse a little too quickly and my cell flipped out of my hand and onto the flagstone floor, shattering into about twelve pieces.

Well, damn. The last thing I wanted to do tomorrow was spend the day at the cell phone store getting a new one. I bent down to pick it up and noticed something right away. It was tiny, it was round, it was silver. And it wasn't supposed to be in my phone.

Just as I was examining it in my hand, Zac and Cassidy came through the kitchen door. Cassidy stopped cold in her tracks when she saw what I was holding. Before she could censor herself, she blurted, "Oh my god!" The look on her face and her unfiltered reaction was all I needed.

"You tapped my phone. How could you? And why? My own daughter? I can't trust my own daughter?"

"I'm not your daughter, I'm your stepdaughter."

"I've never treated you that way. Why did you do this? What information did you think you would get from me?"

"I don't know."

"Where did you get such a device?"

"A friend."

"What kind of friends do you have?"

"Friends with connections."

"But I still don't understand. If you think I'm keeping secrets from you, ask me."

"So you can lie?"

I had to pause after that question. If she did accuse me of having anything to do with her father's death, I would have to lie. I searched back in my memory as thoroughly as I could to try to remember if I'd said anything condemning on my phone. Nothing was coming to me, but it certainly was possible. I looked over at Zac. He looked sickened by the whole conversation. It was clear he had no intention of mediating. No, this was between Cassidy and me.

"Did you hear anything interesting when you were eavesdropping on my personal conversations?"

"Just that you have been gathering the troops a lot lately. You and your Ladies of the Lake have formed quite a tight alliance. Been having a lot of secretive meetings these days. Your phone calls have let me know where and when."

I had to tread carefully. "And did you spy on any of these meetings?"

"Once. I heard some pretty horrible things. The world underestimates you and your gal pals. You come across as wonderful wives and moms. But there's a secret layer to you that is strong, and deadly."

I stayed calm. "No one drove into that door but Hudson."

"Then why do you feel guilty about it?"

"We were in the middle of a terrible fight. I hated him in that moment."

"I know. I loved Daddy. But he was full of himself, above morals, above the law…drunk with alcohol and power. But you didn't handle it with the morals of a saint. I'm leaving in the morning with Zac. We're going to college. My birthday is November 25th. Have my inheritance deposited into my bank account on that day. You will never see me or hear from me again. As for what I'm going to do about Alana, James, and Maddie, well, your cronies will be glad to know I'm not going to do anything. It would destroy them to know what their moms have done to their dads. I wouldn't put them through that hell for anything. They deserve a chance to quietly mourn their fathers. Anything I tell them will just stir up a hornets' nest, and the notoriety of what their moms did will follow them everywhere. I can't ease their pain but I can at least do that for them. So if this does all blow up in your faces and I'm subpoenaed, I won't say anything incriminating about anyone."

Then she turned to Zac, "Let's spend the night at your house. We can finish packing in the morning."

They grabbed each other's hands and headed out. I couldn't think of a damn thing to say. They were probably doing the right thing. I went to the kitchen door and opened it just a crack. They had stopped on my porch, and Cassidy said to Zac, "Well, now you know everything. This is how I want to handle it. Any objections?"

Zac kissed her lightly, "None. Come on, let's go to bed; our lives start in the morning."

And off they went. Cassidy didn't seem to want to seek the total truth but she didn't offer me absolution. I guessed I would have to live with a lack of emotional closure with her for the rest of my life. But there was another kind of closure I needed to get if I was going to really be able to put the past behind me. I knew who Cassidy referred to as "her friend." She'd somehow hooked up with Hudson's mistress. Well that bitch crossed swords with the wrong woman. She obviously knew a little about technology, enough to get a hold of a phone tap. But I was running Hudson's company now. All that education, all those degrees were starting to pay off. I knew what I had to do and I had the money, the power, and the knowledge to do it. I picked up my landline and dialed, "Marty, I know it's late, sorry to bother you, but I need a favor. I've got a phone tap here. Looks state of the art, fresh out of the factory. I will give it to you in the morning and I want you to find where it came from and who bought it."

I listened to Marty make about sixteen excuses as to why that couldn't be done. When I was bored of his whining, I cut him off. "Of course it can be done. Get Fred and Gil to help you. Let's make it fun. A little contest. The guy who finds me the information I need will be promoted to Vice President." I hung up and sunk into a chair, praying they would come up with some answers. This mistress was a wild card I had to take care of. Who knew what she was planning on doing?

CLARA

September 1

32

I CAME OUT OF THE COFFEE shop to find it had started raining hard. Perfect. Of course, I didn't have an umbrella and I'd parked about six blocks from the restaurant. The weather reflected my mood. I had just finished interviewing the last six of Hudson's employees, and I had gotten nowhere. I knew I needed more before I went to the police. For the first time, I doubted my abilities. The thought crossed my mind that I might not bring the truth to light. I had seen it many times as a reporter. Cover-ups happened all the time, and not even the greatest of journalists could always uncover the truth to the satisfaction of the courts. I was jaded and cynical. I'd seen too many guilty people walk free. It now occurred to me that this might happen to Vivian. No one knew of any motive she might have had for killing her husband. To the world, they had a happy and healthy marriage. Only Cassidy and I knew different, and we didn't have enough proof.

I drove to my apartment and let myself in, soaking wet. It was a crappy place to live but I'd gone through all my savings waiting to be with Hudson, and I hadn't worked more than a job or two in months. I was broke.

I sat down on the sofa without bothering to dry off. I looked down at the coffee table and saw Hudson's face staring at me from its frame. I picked up the photo and studied it closely. There was that smile. It always made me weak in the knees. Then I saw a magazine I'd purchased several months ago because it had Hudson's picture on the cover. It was some sort of financial magazine. There it was…that same smile. And it hit me, I had been drawn in by that smile as had the rest of the world. He had always been sweet and charming and charismatic to me, but he came across to everyone that way, even mass media.

All of a sudden the scales fell from my eyes. Yes, Hudson loved me, of that I was sure. But he was used to having his own way. He was not a man of compromise or a man who would stay true to any woman for very long. I knew the trip to Mexico was real. But how long would we have stayed down there before he became bored with me and with our life? I had a *forever* kind of love for Hudson but his, by nature, would have been less enduring.

I dropped to the floor. Knowing Hudson loved me was all I had been living on. Now that was taken away from me. Hopeless, lost, and numb, I went to the kitchen and got out a steak knife. I held it in my right hand for a few minutes and imagined making a slashing motion up my left wrist. I didn't have the courage or the weakness to press metal to flesh, but I took the knife to bed with me that night. I laid it by the pillow should the urge overtake me to end this unendurable pain.

LUPE

September 9

33

I HAD WORKED FOR MR. ROTH for many years. He provided me with a nice maid's room and a good salary. I admit I didn't like his first three wives but I did like the present Mrs. Roth, and I was very troubled by all the terrible things that were happening to her friends. The Ladies often came over to visit. I didn't know their husbands very well, but the Ladies were nice to me.

It was almost two months after Mr. Alphonse's death. It had started out as a normal day. It was a Saturday, so no school. I always dreaded the weekends. The boys came in from having gone paintballing. I saw that they had red and blue and yellow and green paint all over their faces, clothes, and hair. They shrugged out of the paint-smattered overalls they were wearing, threw their eye guards and guns on the floor, and ran upstairs. The paint was still wet in their hair and on their hands, and they were leaving a trail of paint spots all up the stairs. I yelled for them to jump into their showers. They each had their own room with their own bathroom. I doubted they would obey my order, and that frustrated me because I had set aside today to wash all the windows in the house. It was a large house, and the chore would take all day. But it would have to wait for another time as I had a feeling I was going to have to go to the store to try to find some sort of cleaning solvent that would remove paint from walls and carpets, and then spend the rest of the day scrubbing. Because, for once, Mr. Carson was home. He came home late last night and was still asleep. But if he woke to the sight of this, I knew I would be punished instead of the boys.

Mrs. Roth came home in her tennis outfit, racket in hand. She took one look at the paint and then looked at me with sympathy. "Oh Lupe, I'm so sorry."

I told her not to worry about it and then I grabbed my keys and purse, took some of the housekeeping money out of the cookie jar, and headed off to the store.

❧

When I got back, Mr. Roth was clearly awake. I could hear the shouting from the master bedroom. At first, I thought he was mad about the paint but, from what I could make out, he was yelling at Mrs. Roth. She had clearly done something to upset him greatly and I wondered what it could be since they hadn't seen each other in a while.

I have to admit I was curious. So I took my bucket loaded up with various cleaning solutions and decided to start at the top of the stairs. I looked in Wyatt's room. Thank God, he had taken a shower. There was some paint in his room and bathroom, but it wasn't bad. He was playing a video game with his headphones on. I motioned for him to take them off, which he did.

I asked, "Where are the other boys?"

Wyatt said he didn't know, probably the arcade. I peeked inside their rooms, which were covered with drips of paint. This was truly going to be an all-day job.

Wyatt told me, "Dad woke up about an hour ago when Lisa went in to bring him some coffee. They've been yelling at each other ever since. About what, I don't know and don't care. Just don't clean my room now. I'm going to the movies in about half an hour, I have to get away from all this family crap. You can clean in here then." Then he put his headphones back on and turned his attention back to his game.

I started in the hallway, not far from the master suite. As I began scrubbing the walls, I could better hear the fight between the Mr. and the Mrs. In fact, they were so loud, I could hear every word.

"Lisa, I don't want to talk about this anymore. You take care of what needs to be done and don't tell me another word about it."

"How dare you talk to me that way. This is my decision."

"No, it's not. I pay the bills. I decide."

"What are you, some sort of dictator? You didn't always used to talk to me that way. Remember, in the beginning? We actually had two-way conversations. You cared about how I felt and what I thought."

"It's not that I don't care, it's that you're not being rational, so I clearly have to do the thinking for both of us. I don't need this drama, Lisa…I really don't. I've got enough on my hands keeping Jarvis from shooting up 24/7. I don't need drama here at home."

"Well, there's always drama here, thanks to your sons. It's a nightmare. I think that under the current situation, they should all be sent back to live with their mothers. They've got perfectly fine mothers who can take care of them. That's the way to remove drama from this house, not by punishing me."

"Lisa, the way you put things is so ridiculous. I'm not trying to victimize you. I'm trying to get you to see the logic of the situation."

"Shit, Carson, you're talking about logic? Since when have you ever been logical about your drug-addicted, sexually predatory, DUI-acquiring clients?"

"I get them out of trouble, and I keep them out of trouble. And I do that because they pay me. There's nothing more logical than that."

"I'm not generating income for you here, I'm giving you a baby."

I gasped. Mrs. Roth was pregnant?

"Lisa, the last thing we need in this house is another mouth to feed."

"You sound like we're poor or something."

"How did this even happen?"

"I don't know. I think we had sex after you came back from Jarvis's last tour. You were home for two minutes and then gone to babysit Jarvis again. I haven't been on the pill because I thought I was going through menopause. Obviously, I'm not. Look, it happened. We're married. We're having a baby. It happens all the time."

"Not to us it doesn't. One of the things I liked best about you was that you never nagged me about having children. And I figured your biological clock had ticked out, and being a father again was not on my radar."

"Being a mother was never on my radar. But now that I'm pregnant, I'm kind of excited. I thought you would be too."

"Do I seem excited?"

"But it's your baby. Your own flesh and blood. How can you not love it?"

"Are you blind? Have you ever watched me with my three other children. Do I ever really give a crap about them? I let them stay here because I know you and Lupe will keep them out of my hair. It wouldn't be any different with this one. I don't want it. Get rid of it."

"No. If you don't want it, I'll move out."

"You know about our prenup. You won't get a cent from me."

"Mother will help me financially, and I'll sue you for child support."

I peeked around the corner into the bedroom and saw Mr. Roth grab Mrs. Roth by the shoulders. He was squeezing so hard it had to hurt. He pulled her face so close to his.

"Try suing me and I'll come up with a paternity test that proves the baby isn't mine."

"But it is. I haven't been with anybody else."

"I know people. I can make things happen. Trust me, you won't get a dime out of me. Now be a good little wife and go off and get your abortion, and we'll go back to the way things have always been around here, okay?"

He didn't wait for an answer. He threw on his jacket, and I jumped back into Liam's room and hid as he headed down the corridor, stairs, and out the front door. He was so upset he didn't notice all the paint.

I felt sick to my stomach. I left all my cleaning things on the floor and ran down to my room. I barely made it to the bathroom before I threw up. And then I just sat there on the floor and held myself and rocked back and forth, crying. I couldn't help it. I couldn't stop.

I don't know how long this went on before I heard my name being called by Mrs. Roth. I tried to control myself. I wiped my eyes and blew my nose. I struggled to my feet and tried to put a calm expression on my face as I made my way to the kitchen. Mrs. Roth was there looking for me. She had been crying too, but her tears stopped when she saw my face.

"Lupe? What's wrong? You look terrible. Have you been crying?"

"I don't want to concern you, Mrs. Roth."

"Of course I'm concerned. You're part of this family."

"I don't want to take your mind off your own problems."

"What do you mean?"

"I'm sorry, but I heard some of what you and Mr. Roth said to each other. You're going to have a baby?"

"Not if Mr. Roth has anything to say about it."

"I'm just the housekeeper. But I hope you keep the baby, even if it means you have to move out. I could go with you to your mother's."

"That's sweet of you, Lupe. But I don't know what I'm going to do. Mr. Roth can be a very persuasive man."

"You mean you're thinking about getting rid of the baby?"

"Yes."

"But you can't."

"Look, I know you come from El Salvador and that you have very strong religious beliefs, but I don't share those beliefs. If the timing isn't right, it's just not right."

Tears started spilling out of my eyes. "Señora, it's not about timing, it's about you, what you want, how you really feel. How far along are you?"

"I'm not sure. I just took a home pregnancy test. I haven't been to see the doctor yet. And my periods have been irregular. I thought I was just gaining weight because I'd stopped exercising. With all that's been going on with my friends at the club, I haven't been sticking to my regular routine. It didn't even occur to me until yesterday that I might be pregnant."

I took Mrs. Roth by the hand and led her into the living room where we both sat down. I had something to tell her. Something I swore I would never tell anyone. But I knew then it was God's will that I tell her my most shameful secret.

So I told her about many years ago when I worked for Mr. Roth and he was married to the third Mrs. Roth, and she was expecting little Liam. It was a difficult pregnancy and she required bed rest. Mr. Roth was upset that such a fuss was being made. He said he was a man who had needs and he needed sex. Mrs. Roth said she was sorry but the baby came first.

"It was in Mrs. Roth's eighth month that he first came to me. He came into my room when I was in bed. It was dark. I was very frightened. He told me not to be silly, just to think of it as part of the job.

"I had never had such an important man approach me that way. I was not a virgin, but I was not very experienced either. I must have pleased him because he came to my room many times after that first night. Even after Liam was born and Mrs. Roth needed her rest, he came to me. Until one day, I told him I was pregnant. I was afraid he was going to fire me. And indeed he was very angry. He told me he would fire me if I did not have an abortion. I knew if I kept the baby, there would be no way for me to get another job with my own child to care for. So I did as he said. Afterwards I had to come home and take care of baby Liam. My heart broke into a million pieces every time I rocked him or fed him or held him. I thought of my little boy or girl who I could never hold, never touch, never love. I cried a lot when I cared for Liam, it was so painful. But I was careful. I hid my tears. After a while, the pain lessened. But I go to bed every night knowing I'm going to burn in hell for what I did. I have always secretly hated Mr. Roth for what he made me do. I would have left him but he married you. And you were so nice, I wanted to stay. But you must never do what he made me do."

"You're not going to burn in hell, even if there is such a place, which

I doubt. And neither will I. But I am so sorry my husband did that to you. I'm so sorry he made you go through such pain."

"He is not a good man."

"No. I realize that now. I guess I've known that for a long time. But he is powerful, and I don't know what to do. I may have to give up this baby. I'll sleep on it and decide in the morning."

She left, and I stood and raised my fist in the air towards God and promised him Mrs. Roth would not have to make that decision.

After I'd cleaned up all the paint and fixed dinner, I called for Mrs. Roth and the children to be seated at the dining table. There was the usual fighting between the boys, but Mrs. Roth was so deep inside her own thoughts that she didn't notice. I brought out dessert and suggested to Mrs. Roth that she call one of her friends, talk this over with them. She shook her head and said no. She didn't want anyone to know about this. I told her I respected that. And I promised that I wouldn't tell a soul.

Then, I went to my room and called an old boyfriend of mine in Palmdale. He thought I was calling to get back together, but that wasn't it at all. I needed a favor. He could hook me up with a good drug dealer, couldn't he? Miguel said that, of course, he could. I told him what I needed. He said no problem. He felt bad for breaking up with me and felt like he owed me. He'd find a reliable pusher and do it all for free. I thanked him, hung up, grabbed my rosary, and started to pray for the sin I was about to commit.

Two hours later, Miguel called back. All went according to plan. The pusher knocked on the door to the hotel room where Mr. Roth was keeping watch over his client, Jarvis. Jarvis answered the door and informed the pusher that Mr. Roth was in the bathroom. Seizing the opportunity, the pusher offered Jarvis some high grade heroin. The singer said yes and immediately shot up and sank into oblivion. The pusher called in a friend, and when Mr. Roth came out of the bathroom, the two men held him down on a sofa and injected him with a lethal dose. It was a piece of cake. No one saw them go in. No one saw them go out.

I thanked Miguel over and over again. Then I hung up the phone and cried tears of joy.

DETECTIVE SHAUN DANIELS

September 10

34

THE LAST PLACE IN THE WORLD I wanted to be was sitting at my desk. The teasing and torment had gone on all day. It started off with Detective Mirano coming by and saying, "Shaun, big news at the country club. They just lost another one. Seems one of the sand traps had been replaced with quicksand, and one of the golfers was just swallowed into the ground. Better get over there and check on it."

I wasn't amused.

The other guys couldn't lay off either. Detective Jackson ran up to my desk flapping his arms, "Oh dear. One of the golfers was found dead in the middle of the ninth fairway with a tee stuck in his eyeball. Sounds suspiciously like foul play to me. Don't you think you'd better check it out?"

Hollister was at the desk next to me. He'd been given all the files on all the unfortunate events that had taken place with the group of golf buddies at Avalon. I told him he wasn't going to find anything. And the only thing that remotely seemed like foul play was Alphonse Louis' death with the gun. But Hollister wasn't looking at me, he was busy poring over garage door repair reports, medical information about Viagra overdosing, every piece of background information he could get about Sheraton's private life, and all known enemies or competitors of Alphonse Louis. He actually had some luck there. There had been some talk in town that Alphonse was up for a very big movie role, and he had the inside track. Then bam, Alphonse is dead and some guy ten years younger comes out of nowhere and gets the role. Motive? Maybe. But Hollister was going to have to dig a lot deeper.

Meanwhile, I was sick of the whole thing. I had a knot in the pit of my stomach that I only get when I have a feeling…a hunch that turns out to be right. I knew it wouldn't be long before Hollister came up with the same theory I was starting to form. I was still lead detective on this. I had to do something. The problem was, it involved a woman I was starting to love.

I grabbed my jacket. I had to get out of here. The very not-funny jokes were really starting to get to me, and I needed to talk to Crystal. But before I could get out the door, the captain walked up and said, "We've got another dead golfer on our hands."

"Look, Cap…I have taken all the crap I can handle. So if you'll stop being a comedian for about five minutes, I'd like to go out and do my job."

"I'm not shitting you. Carson Roth was found dead in a hotel in Beverly Hills. He had apparently been babysitting one of his more troubled clients, a heroin addict slash rock star. This morning they were both found unconscious, with needle marks in their arms, and needles all over the place. The rock star is okay. But Roth overdosed. He's as dead as the rest of his buddies."

Hollister joined us, "What's this?"

The captain was in a foul mood. "Five dead guys…okay, one technically only missing. Stop looking for outside motives. Even though most of their deaths looked like accidents or products of their bizarre lifestyles, we have to focus on one thing. That fucking country club. I mean, what are the odds of five best golfing buddies going like that so close to each other? I want you guys to scour that club inside and out. Get to know every worker. Question the families again and again and again. We've got nothing so far on any of these deaths. No forensic proof that they died as a result of foul play. But come on…fucking Nancy Drew would have solved this by now. I don't know if we're dealing with one guy who wanted to off these boys or what, but we've got to find out. And I need hard evidence. Something I can take to a judge. And I want it fast. No more goofing around."

I saw red. "Goofing around? We didn't even know these events were connected until now, and we're still not sure how they are or if they are. I've been doing my damn job, Cap, and if you don't think so, make Hollister the lead detective of the case. He's an idiot, but he'll come up with some bullshit solution to the case. Look, his fucking socks don't even match."

I slammed out of the precinct office more pissed off than I've ever been.

35

I DIDN'T EVEN KNOCK WHEN I rolled through Crystal's front door. She'd stopped locking it ever since Jonathan died. I don't know why. You think she'd feel less safe. But she just sort of floated through life, and she felt cozy with her little women's entourage living so close by.

Crystal had the TV on the news and was talking on the phone at the same time. I stepped back into the foyer. I'm not a big fan of over-hearing conversations but I was pretty mad, and most of my scruples had gone out the window on the drive over.

"Lisa, it's Crystal. I just turned on the news and there it was. I had no idea Carson did drugs. This couldn't have come at a worse time. What are we going to do?"

I stepped into the room, "That's a very good question."

Startled, Crystal whipped around. She started trembling with fear at the sight of me. She kept her eyes on me but spoke into the phone, "Lisa, I'll have to call you back."

She hung up. She clearly didn't know what to say. She didn't want to talk first so she went and poured herself a cup of coffee to buy time.

"Want some?"

"No."

"You sound…um…terse."

"Yeah, no need for caffeine for me. I've had about all the stimulation for one morning I can handle. Just tell me one thing. And if you're not honest, I'll know it. Were you playing me?"

"What do you mean?"

"You know what I mean. The flirting, the dinner. It was all on the up and up for me. But since five out of six of your girlfriends' husbands are dead…"

"Not Sheraton."

I slammed my fist on the kitchen table. "No more games. I'm sure he's dead."

"Don't you have to have a body to prove that?"

"What are you, an expert on crime?"

"No, but…"

"Shut up and listen to me. I will not be made a fool of. And I will not let five murders go unsolved on my watch."

I was interrupted by a phone call on my cell. I listened for a moment then hung up.

"So the gun that killed Alphonse did not have the blanks replaced with real bullets, it was an entirely different gun. That means the killer knew what the gun was going to look like. Who would have information like that?"

"Why are you asking me? I guess someone who worked on the show."

"Don't do that. Don't bullshit me. There's something between us, Crystal. Something…I don't know. I can't read your mind, but I can read your eyes. Those green eyes are like a window to your soul. Of course, the cast and crew are going to be questioned again, but my money is on someone from Avalon. Too many coincidences. And, as

I told you once before, I don't believe in coincidences. You have five best girlfriends. Four of their husbands, including your own, are dead. Bam, bam, bam, bam, bam…just like that. On the surface, it looks like these crimes have nothing to do with each other. In fact, on the surface, except for Alphonse, none of them look like crimes at all. But they are. They have to be. There's no way this could just be a string of bad luck you and your wealthy buddies are going through. What gives, Crystal? What are you ladies up to?"

Crystal melted down into the dining chair. I wanted to hate her as I was pretty sure she'd been sent by the others to keep me distracted. I had no proof of this, but I could feel the guilt radiating from her body.

Still my heart melted a little and my anger dissipated. I sat in the chair next to her. "I know there's not a mean bone in your body, honey. I also know what a prick your husband was. In fact, the more I looked into the lives of the dead men, the more I realized they were all pricks. I'm sure you and your girlfriends traded happy lives for money when you all married your husbands. But did it become so bad that it turned you into killers? I can't believe that either. I don't know what to believe. Help me out here. Not just for me, I don't give a crap if there's a black mark on my record because I blew this case, I have to know because after Hollister goes through all the info I've been through, he's going to come to the same conclusion…even though he's a dolt. I don't have a shred of proof of what I'm accusing you of, but I know you and your pals had something to do with all this. And I want to protect you. But I can't if you don't trust me."

Crystal mustered up some strength, "I don't know as much about my friends as you think. But I can tell you this and it's the God's honest truth. Lisa had nothing to do with Carson's death. He died just as he appeared to…a drug overdose. Question her, you'll see."

"Why is it that you go straight to declaring Lisa's innocence, but not your own?"

"My husband was sixty-five years old and he had way too much sex with way too many partners, and the only way he could keep up with his voracious appetite was to take too much Viagra. That's what killed my husband. Jonathan boasted to me he was expecting to have sex with a third girl in our bed the day after I had my miscarriage. I was raw. I was in agony that I would never have a child. If my asshole husband wanted to sleep with countless women in my bed, I made sure it was going to happen. I gave him enough little blue pills to screw half of Beverly Hills. I was angry, but I didn't know it was going to kill him. If you want to take me to the DA and have charges pressed against me, go ahead. But there's no case there. You and I know it. All you'll do is lose me forever."

Crystal was sobbing now. I wanted to comfort her but she had just sort of confessed to helping Jonathan to his grave. Was it murder? I believed her when she said she didn't know those extra pills were going to kill him. I had to get away from her before I took her in my arms, because once I did that, I know I'd never have the strength to let go. So I backed away, told her to calm down. I wasn't going to do anything now except talk to Lisa. I would see her later.

I left Crystal's house hating my job.

☙

Lisa opened her door looking like a woman who'd just lost her husband. It was clear she'd been crying all morning. She invited me in with no hesitation, no sense of hiding something or guilt or any red flag that would indicate that she was anything but a grieving widow. She was quite willing and ready to talk, though she had to blow her nose and dab at her eyes every once in a while.

"I just found out this morning. I found out the same way everyone else did, on the news. Carson hadn't been home much ever since Jarvis came to town. Carson felt it was his personal responsibility to keep his client clean. I can't believe Jarvis convinced Carson to join him in his heroin taking or whatever you call it. And the hell of it all is that Jarvis, who has nearly overdosed a thousand times, is going to be fine. And the one time the stuff enters my husband's system, it kills him."

"Maybe you didn't know your husband as well as you thought you did. Addicts are very clever at hiding their problems. Needles can be inserted between toes and fingers; there are lots of ways to hide tracks."

"Yes, but we're talking about heroin here. You met my husband. Did he seem like the kind of guy who would do heroin? Cocaine, maybe. He always went a hundred miles an hour."

"Sometimes people mix to balance out."

"Look, I'm not going to argue with you. Do an autopsy. You will find one needle mark on him. The one that killed him."

"Did you ever visit the hotel where he and this Jarvis person stayed?"

"No, Carson was very firm on the division of his two worlds. Business would never cross paths with his family life and vice versa. And I didn't have any trouble with that. It was important to shield the children from the horrible people he had for clients. But you have to understand, Carson got off on saving these troubled people from themselves, not joining them in their vices. This death makes no sense."

"I'll try to get surveillance footage from the hotel lobby, see if anyone sketchy came in."

"Of course someone sketchy came in and sold them heroin. How else do you think they got the stuff?"

"No need to be snarky with me, Mrs. Roth. I've got very little to go on here."

"I'm sorry. Maybe it's the shock of Carson's death plus hormones. I'm going to have a baby."

"A baby?"

"Yes, I know it seems very biblical, but a woman my age can get pregnant."

"I'm sorry, I meant no disrespect."

"Now maybe you can understand why this is doubly painful for me. I have to raise a fatherless child."

"Speaking of kids, where are his other sons?"

"Gone to stay with their own mothers. The little hellions. The minute I found out about Carson, I sent the brats packing. When you look into my personal affairs, you'll see that Carson and I had an airtight prenup. I'll get no money. The money will go to his sons. Not even a cent will go to this baby. So I'll be moving out of the house shortly. But don't fret. I can take care of myself and my baby."

"Since the children are gone, is there no one left in the house I can question? Didn't you have a housekeeper?"

Lisa stiffened a bit. "I sent Lupe away. I gave her some money and told her to seek employment elsewhere. I don't know where she went."

"You seem more upset about Lupe leaving than the kids."

"Lupe was loyal and wonderful to me."

"Why'd you send her away so quickly? Surely you could have kept her on a few more weeks to help with the transition and the packing."

"I told you, I couldn't pay her. She offered to stay on for nothing. She was just that wonderful, but I couldn't let her do that. I know she had a lead on another job. I'm not sure where or with whom, but I wanted her to take it while it was still available."

"I won't trouble you today anymore, Mrs. Roth. I'm very sorry for your loss, but I am happy for you and the baby."

"Thank you."

I walked to my car more confused than ever. Crystal was right. Lisa had nothing to do with her husband's death, I was sure of it. But there had to be a connection to the other deaths.

I decided to head back over to Crystal's. I wasn't sure what I was going to say to her. If I shook her down hard enough, I would get it out of her that she knew about the other deaths, but she would never give me details. And if I had to be harsh with her…well, that would be the end of us or any chance of us in the future.

Still uncertain of how to play my next move, my cell rang just as I got to Crystal's front walkway. It was Hollister. He said some woman had been calling my desk phone over and over again since I left. She sounded a little whacky. She only wanted to talk to me. He wasn't about to give her my cell number, but she kept saying she had information about the Avalon cases and mumbled something about Carson and Hudson. Frankly, Hollister wouldn't have given her the time of day but she was so persistent, he took down her number. I could call her if I wanted to, but it sounded like a waste of time to him.

I hung up and knew what I had to do. It was the only lead I'd had and whacko or not, I had to follow it. Also, it bought me time to figure out how best to deal with Crystal.

Hollister had texted me the woman's phone number so I dialed it. She sounded edgy and a little inebriated. I could see why Hollister didn't want to take her seriously. She asked me if I knew about Carson. I told her of course I did. She said she knew without a doubt that all five men from the Avalon club had been victims of their own wives. She had compelling proof. She wanted to meet me at the top of a parking garage in downtown. I asked her why I just couldn't go to her place, but she seemed very skittish and more than a little distrustful of cops in general. I tried to sound as reassuring as possible, wrote down the address, and told her I'd be there in half an hour.

36

FOR SEPTEMBER, IT WAS A BIT chilly and windy at the top of the partially covered parking structure. A steady rain was falling. There were only about half a dozen cars parked on this level. I pulled into one of the many open spaces and looked around wondering, what the hell I was getting myself into?

I spotted her right away, from the back. She was tall, lanky, with a bright red wool sweater and wool pants. The weather called for a coat, which she wasn't wearing, but she wasn't shivering either. As I shut my car door, she turned. She was very beautiful. At first, I thought Scandinavian. But when she spoke, I heard more of an Eastern European accent which I couldn't quite place. Her hair was straight, blonde, and cut bluntly at the chin line. It was whipping all over in the wind.

"Thank you for coming."

"Will you make it worth my while?"

"Yes."

"What do you have for me?"

"Proof that all the men from the Avalon Country Club that met with untimely ends were the victims of foul play. They were all killed by their own wives."

"What about Sheraton?"

"I'm sure he is dead somewhere."

"What's your interest in this case?"

"I was in love with Hudson Montgomery. He was going to leave his wife for me. She never would have let that happen."

"So she dropped a garage door on him? Sounds a little farfetched. Although, I have had my own suspicions about the wives."

"I knew I couldn't prove it so I waited. Then another husband died, then another disappeared, then another died, and another. Now they're all gone. When I heard about Mr. Roth this morning, I knew I had to contact the police before the trail grew too cold."

"What's your name?"

"Clara."

"What do you do for a living?"

"I'm a journalist. I had an affair with Hudson for many months. We loved each other deeply. We couldn't stand to be away from each other. The night Hudson broke the news to his wife was the night he died. I know she did it."

"Forget about what you know. What can you prove?"

"A woman in my business is able to get her hands on many useful tools. I tapped Vivian's cell phone."

"You know that's illegal."

"Yes, I just thought I might hear something that might lead to something substantial that I could take to the police."

"Not that it's admissible, but can I hear what you got?"

Clara pulled out a small recording device and played a series of abrupt calls Vivian made. Each time, she summoned Crystal, Lisa, Morgan, and Anjelica, and every time, excluded Dorothy. The recordings ended after about five or six of these kinds of calls.

"There were other calls, of course. But they had nothing to do with the case, so I edited them out."

"So what you're telling me is you have a series of calls the taping of which are all illegal. And all the calls tell us is that five girlfriends get together on a regular basis. You're a journalist. You know this is worthless. How did you even get close enough to Vivian to put a tap on her phone?"

"I enlisted the help of her stepdaughter, Cassidy."

"You're kidding? Why would you put it into Cassidy's head that her stepmother might have killed her dad? What kind of cruel mind game is that?"

"She has no love for her stepmother, and she wanted to know the truth as much as I did. I supplied her with the tap and she placed it in the phone. Those were all the relevant calls we heard before Vivian found the tap. She's quite the little techno-wiz. She knows what I was trying to do. That's why I insisted we meet up here."

"What do you have besides these recordings?"

"Cassidy hid and listened in on one of these meetings. She heard many incriminating things, actual confessions. I've got it all written down."

She tried to hand me a spiral bound notebook, but I batted it away. "I'm not going to read that. It's all hearsay. Is Cassidy willing to testify to what she heard?"

"Unfortunately not. She's firm on that. She is a smart one. She knows we don't have any hard evidence, that bringing all this to light will just tarnish her father's name. But I say we dig a little deeper. Connect the dots between Hudson's death and the others. There's got to be some bit of something tangible out there that could blow this thing open."

She swayed a little on her feet. I could hear the rain coming down harder.

"Have you been drinking?"

"Of course I have. My life is ruined. I lost the love of my life. I was willing to give up everything for him. Now I have no one, no job, nothing to live for except revenge. I'm not stupid, Detective Daniels. I know this is not enough to take to the DA, but if you will just read the notebook, it might give you an idea about where to look next…some sort of lead. I wrote down everything Cassidy overheard one night when the Ladies were talking. It's very detailed. Here take it."

I was touched by the grief and desolation in her eyes. "Okay, give me the notebook, I'll read through it." Of course, my first thought was Crystal, and what I might find out about her part in all this.

Suddenly Clara pulled the book back. "No. This was a mistake. You police have been two steps behind these women all along. Maybe you don't want to arrest them. Maybe this will get so bogged down that it will never see the inside of a courtroom." She lifted up the notebook. "I have no copy of this. I'd better keep it. I don't trust you."

I blocked the way to her car. I could easily overpower her and get the book. I hoped it wasn't going to come to that.

"I need that book, Clara. If these women are guilty, I'll use the book to find hard evidence. But I need it."

"No. I'm going to hire a private detective. He'll dig up the dirt."

She swayed on her feet. She was obviously at the end of her rope. She was drunk, and her eyes were filled with anger and pain. This woman was clearly intelligent and wise. But bitter, desperate thoughts had warped her mind and alcohol had numbed her self-control. She took a step backwards.

"I'm not letting you have this. I'm not. Hudson's death will be avenged, but not by you. You're just some stupid cop who has allowed a string of murders to happen right in front of your nose, and you haven't done anything about it." She held the notebook tightly to her chest. "You'll never do anything with this either." She took another step back.

"Give it to me or I'll place you under arrest for obstruction of justice."

"You can't arrest me. You can't bring Hudson back to life. Nothing good is ever going to come of this. But Vivian won't win. She won't have Hudson. I will."

I started to panic. "What do you mean?"

Her answer was to turn and run to a low barrier at the edge of the structure. It was easily twelve floors down to the street. I ran for her and grabbed her around the waist. She struggled, twisted, and turned, but I wasn't going to let her go. I was about ready to carry her over to my car when she produced a pistol out of her coat pocket. Before I had time, she shot. She missed, even at that close of range. She was too out of control to shoot straight. But the sight and sound of the gun threw me, and I loosened my grip just a little. She pushed out my arms, and the momentum of that push sent her back over the barrier and off the side of the structure.

I yelled, "No!" But it was too late. She was falling. I watched her land and knew the fall had killed her instantly. I ran down the stairs of the parking lot to her body. Several horrified people watched as I approached. Two were on their cell phones calling 911. I looked around frantically for the notebook. It didn't take me long to see it. It was floating away from her in a gutter leading to the opening of a storm drain. The rain was pouring over it. Before I could retrieve it, it was swept away into the city's main sewer system.

37

I WAS BACK AT THE STATION filling out my report when Captain Harris called me into his office. I was not in the best of moods, but the captain looked even worse.

"I have some bad news, Daniels."

"What could that possibly be?"

"Some teenage guy down on the sidewalk saw you and that woman struggling. He didn't get the first part of it, but he started taping on his cell as soon as he saw you two struggle."

"We were fighting over something. It will all be in my report."

"Indulge me now."

"It was a notebook."

"What did it contain?"

I realized that the captain was treating me like a suspect. My walls went up. "I don't know. She just said it had to do with the Montgomery case. It fell into a storm drain. We had to retrieve it from the sewer so it's very degraded—virtually destroyed. It's in the lab right now. I doubt they'll be able to decipher it."

The captain put his feet up and wiped his hands over his face as if he were disgusted. "Meanwhile, we still have to deal with this kid on the street."

"I don't follow."

"As I said, when he saw you struggling with the woman, he took his phone out and recorded it. Want to see it?"

"Not particularly."

The captain took his feet down anyway, grabbed a remote control, and turned on the TV that sat across from his desk. There was the image of Clara and myself. You couldn't hear us but we were certainly involved in some physical contact, then you could hear a gunshot. When it came to the part where she fell, I instinctively leaned out, trying to grab her. I don't remember doing that, but the whole thing was kind of a blur. Cap turned off the TV.

"So?"

"So it kind of looks like you pushed her."

"You're shitting me."

"Not at all."

"Why would I have pushed her?"

"I don't know. But Internal Affairs is looking into it and until I get a report from them, I have to take your badge and gun. As of now, you're on leave."

"This is bullshit."

"Maybe. But it looks bad. We can't have people videotaping our officers pushing people off buildings."

"She wasn't just people, she was Hudson Montgomery's mistress."

"Let me guess, she accused Mrs. Montgomery of killing her husband with a garage door. And she jotted down her little suspicion in her little book."

"She called the meeting to give me the book but at the last minute, she changed her mind. I wanted that book and we fought over it. Then she went nuts about her dead boyfriend and took a shot at me and fell."

"It didn't look like she fell."

"She'd been drinking. And she was crazed with grief, but she was no ordinary woman. She was a professional journalist."

"I don't care if she'd won a Pulitzer. Getting your claws on the diary of a madwoman is hardly worth throwing her off a building."

"I didn't throw anybody anywhere. And this is the first break in this case we've had. Ever since Louis died, we've all felt the Avalon deaths were somehow connected. This notebook would have connected the dots."

"Were they confessions?"

"No. Clara enlisted the help of Vivian Montgomery's stepdaughter. Cassidy bugged her mom's phone, then listened in on a little party the Ladies of the Lake were having. She heard some innuendo and some planning."

"You come in here with an illegal phone tap and a book of gossip we can't even read. Daniels, what's wrong with you? If these Avalon cases are connected, you've done a damn poor job of filling in the blanks."

"There are a lot of unanswered questions and no hard evidence in any of the cases. You think Hollister can do better, good luck to him. You might want to give him a heads-up that I don't think Sheraton Firestone ran off. I'm pretty sure he's as dead as Alphonse, Hudson, Jonathan, and Carson. But Hollister won't be able to find proof of that either. It will be interesting watching all of you chase your tails."

I pulled my gun out of my shoulder holster and put it on the desk. Then I reached in my inside jacket pocket and got my badge. I threw that on the desk too.

The captain looked real upset. "I.A. is not happy about this. The press got a hold of the footage of you and that Clara woman. It's a publicity nightmare. I wouldn't be surprised if the commissioner insisted on your termination."

"Then fuck all of you," I said. I didn't bother clearing out my desk or saying goodbye to anyone. I just left the building and headed straight for the first bar I could find.

After my fourth double bourbon, I got a call from the lab saying the notebook was useless. As soon as I hung up, I got a call from the captain, who had just finished reading I.A.'s report. I was watching myself and Clara on the bar's TV when I was notified that I was fired. I figured this called for another drink, and another, and another. Until everything went black.

⁂

The next morning I woke up in my own bed, not sure how I got there. I put myself together as best I could. The cold shower felt good but shaving seemed too labor intensive. I got in my car and headed over to the Montgomery house. I might not have a job but I wanted answers, just for my own peace of mind.

Vivian opened the door. Crystal was with her. Vivian said she was about to put her coat on and head to work.

"Yeah, kind of nice the way that all worked out. You inheriting your husband's company."

Vivian was cool as a snake as she slipped into her Burberry raincoat. "Yes, and I'm running it a helluva lot better than he did. Can I help you, Detective?"

"Don't call me that."

Crystal had a panicked sound in her voice. "Why not?"

"Because I no longer work for the L.A.P.D. This is just a courtesy call. I wanted to tell you, Mrs. Montgomery, that your late husband's mistress is dead."

Vivian's expression didn't change a bit. She was cool and calm. "I'm not going to pretend I didn't know about her. I saw the little tussle you had with her in that parking garage on the news. I suppose that's why you were fired."

"I didn't push her."

"Nevertheless, I had every intention of sending you a note. Now I can tell you in person. Thank you. Now, I suppose you two have a lot to talk about. Just lock up when you leave." And she was out the door.

Crystal and I just stood there. We didn't make eye contact, we didn't move at all. Finally Crystal spoke up. "Did you get in trouble because…I mean…did I have anything to do…Did you do anything for me that might have got you in trouble?"

"No. My boss thinks I pushed someone off a roof. There will be an investigation but that video footage is inconclusive. They won't charge me with anything. I'm not going to jail. I'm just out of a job."

Crystal laughed.

"That's funny?"

"Sort of. You're unemployed and I'm broke. What a pair we make."

"What are you talking about?"

"You told me if I were to have any chance with you, I'd have to give up Jonathan's money. So that's what I did. I divided it up and made huge donations to several charities. I'm even moving out of the house on Saturday. I found a nice little apartment on Fountain Avenue."

"You did that for me?"

"I did it for us."

I took her in my arms and suddenly, the crappiest week I'd ever had turned into the best I ever had.

🙟

The next night Morgan was throwing Crystal a goodbye party, which I thought was ludicrous since she was only moving twenty minutes away. But Crystal told me it was the end of an era. Her pals loved her but now that she was broke, she would never be one of them again. She swore she didn't mind because she claimed she belonged to me now. But still, to her, a party seemed appropriate. She begged me to go as her escort, a suggestion I found highly ridiculous since, up until a day ago, I was investigating them.

It took Crystal pulling me into the shower with her that morning to convince me to go with her. What the hell. We had spent all night having sex and I was stupid, crazy in love with her, so she could have just about talked me into anything. What I didn't tell her is that you don't just stop being a cop overnight. They can take your gun and badge away, but they can't take your instinct and your naturally inquisitive nature. I was going, but I was not going to relax around these people.

Crystal went through my closet and declared that I didn't have anything to wear. I thought all my clothes were fine, but she dragged me to Neiman Marcus and made me buy a new suit. I wasn't broke. I'd saved quite a bit of money, but it was going to go fast if she had me buy stuff this expensive. She promised to go on a budget after this one spree, but I confess to being a little grouchy about having to put on some pretentious clothes and pretend I was something I'm not.

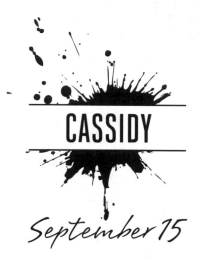

CASSIDY

September 15

38

I HAD A STRANGE FEELING OF life coming full circle when Zac and I walked, hand in hand, into the clubhouse dining room for Crystal's party. We had debated whether we wanted to go or not, especially after all the macabre incidents that had happened. But at the last minute, we decided to hop on a plane and come down from Oregon just for the night. We both had tests coming up so we needed to leave first thing in the morning.

I saw my stepmom. She smiled and headed for me, but I turned around and went the other way. I was just not ready to talk to her. I'm not sure I'll ever be ready.

Zac headed straight for his parents. I joined them. I must say that for two people who never seemed to quite fit in at the club, they looked amazing. They still never quite got the fashion thing. Tommy was in a baggy Hawaiian shirt and khaki shorts, and Dotty was sporting a colorful, strapless dress definitely designed for someone about twenty years younger, with less saggy boobs. Zac hugged his parents and told them he had good news. He'd gotten a job selling tickets at a movie theatre to take the pressure off them having to pay for his tuition. Dotty assured him he didn't have to do that. But Tommy was proud of his son for getting a job and paying for part of his life.

Then they dropped their big news. They were moving. The Avalon house was really too big for just the two of them, and they really enjoyed Vegas. Dotty's smile flattened out to give her expression a somewhat bitter look.

"Besides, we never really felt accepted here anyway."

I hugged her and assured her that no one looked down on her. And I really meant it. She wasn't in the inner circle, but the Ladies had always enjoyed her colorful presence at social events.

Despite the joy at seeing his son, you could see deep-seated pain in Tommy's eyes as he hoarsely whispered, "Besides, this place isn't the same. I don't even play golf anymore. I just can't. Not without... them." He wiped a tear from his eye, and Dotty and Zac comforted him. I wanted to give them a moment of privacy so I moved through the room trying to find another familiar face.

I spotted Margaret and Lisa. I gave the old woman a tender hug. "Mags, you look wonderful. Younger every day."

"I love the way you lie, my dear."

I turned to Lisa. "Look at you. Look at that bump."

She had turned from the most neurotic and edgy woman in the world to the most serene. "The baby's kicking a little. I wish you could feel it. A couple more weeks and then when the kicks are stronger, I'm going to give everyone full access to touching my stomach. I'm so happy about this baby. I want everyone to share in the joy."

All my theories as to the part the wives played in their husband's misfortunes had been set aside, and I had no regrets. Lisa was so happy that I just couldn't judge. I just wanted life to move on. And the birth of this baby was surely an omen of good times ahead. I hugged her fiercely. "I couldn't be happier for you."

I saw Morgan and Anjelica in the corner of the room giving some instructions to the waiters. I skipped over to them and gave them both a hug. It hadn't been more than a month since I saw them last, but it seemed like forever. They looked so rested, tan, and lovely, I had to comment, "You both look ten years younger. What's your secret?"

Anjelica winked and said, "We'll never tell."

Morgan lightly punched her in the arm, "Don't be so obtuse. We took a little trip to Cape Cod, that's all."

"Well, the trip certainly did agree with you both."

Our attention was distracted by a smattering of applause. I turned to see Crystal walk in on the arm of Detective Daniels. I had heard rumors that they were together but one look at them, and you could tell they were *together*. They couldn't keep their eyes or hands off of each other. I could tell Daniels was nervous but Crystal's exuberance rubbed off on him, and she floated through the room all huggy and kissy until finally I could see Daniels relax a little.

There were a lot more people there at the party than I knew, and the room was wall-to-wall well-wishers. Crystal was very popular. I could almost picture my father, Jonathan, Alphonse, and Carson standing on the balcony, smoking cigars and giving each other grief for the bad round of golf they'd played earlier that day. I felt a tug on my sleeve and turned to see that Daniels had separated from Crystal.

"Thinking about your dad?"

"Yeah. How'd you know?"

"If I were you, I'd be doing the same thing."

"I'm sorry you lost your job."

"I'm sorry about Clara. I really am. I never wanted her to get hurt. She was pretty messed up that day. I didn't push her. You know that, don't you?"

"Yeah. It's not in your nature to do something like that. What were you fighting over, anyway?"

"She had me listen to the tape of the recordings you made from your stepmom's phone. Then, she showed me a notebook where she'd written very specific notes on what you reported to her about all your stepmom's friends and how they might be connected with the men's deaths."

"Did you ever get a look at it?"

"No. She took it over the side with her. It was destroyed when she fell."

"It wasn't much. But still, I'm not gonna tell you what was in it."

"I'm not gonna ask."

"Okay then." I was going to tell him how happy I was that he and Crystal hooked up and how I always hated Jonathan, but James and Maddie came running into the room and wrapped their arms around me. Daniels left to give us some space.

Maddie was grinning from ear to ear. "I can't believe you came."

James seemed equally happy. "Yeah, I thought we wouldn't see you and Zac until Thanksgiving."

"We wanted to be here. How are you guys doing?"

James was honest. His smile faded. "Good days and bad days. I miss Dad."

Maddie was in agreement. "Yeah. It's not having the closure, you know. That's the hardest part. But Mom's been great."

I saw Zac approaching. "You guys have the money to go anywhere you want and yet you both decided to go to college locally? Don't you want to get out there in the world and do stuff?"

James shook his head. "We want to stay where it's warm and dry. For now, we're happy here."

I saw Crystal speaking intently with Tommy and Dotty. She hugged them both. Tommy had tears in his eyes again. Then Crystal went to the bar, got a martini, and went to search for her date. When she found him talking to Margaret, she pulled him away, a worried look on her face. She pulled him out of the room and onto the balcony. Zac, Maddie, and James wanted to split and head to our favorite hideout behind the club. I told them to go ahead, I'd meet up with them later. I was super curious as to what was going on with Crystal and Daniels. I went downstairs, through the kitchen, and out the side door. I rounded the corner to the front of the clubhouse and right underneath the balcony.

I could hear everything they said.

Crystal spoke first. "I have to talk to you. I've been talking to the girls, and we need to get together one more time. I think there are some loose ends that need tying up before some of us move. It's going to be the last official meeting of the Ladies of the Lake and we want you to be there tomorrow, late morning."

"Why?"

"Just come. It's kind of important."

"What do you mean 'kind of?'"

"I need closure on this part of my life. We're splitting up the group since I'm moving in with you and apparently, Dot and Tommy are leaving. We gal pals have never invited a man to one of our gatherings. Feel honored and join us. You might even learn a thing or two."

"I don't think I want to learn any more than I already know. I'm not a cop any longer and…"

"…I know. Just do it. I promise you that you'll be glad you did."

I was so frustrated. All that sneaking around and I hadn't learned a thing. Except Crystal wanted to bring her boyfriend to a pre-lunch wine party. Still, the invite in itself was odd and my curiosity rebounded.

39

I HAD A HARD TIME CONVINCING Zac to change our flights to late the next evening. I didn't want to tell him why. For some reason, I felt like I needed to know what was going on but I didn't think he'd approve if he knew I was snooping. I gave him some song and dance about wanting private time with my stepmom to try to build a bridge. He realized it would give him a little more time with Tommy and Dot. So he made the change in our flight plans.

The next day, I left my house (once again without speaking to Vivian) to head over to Crystal's. It was only about eleven in the morning, but I knew the wine would be flowing freely. I was hoping it would loosen some tongues that otherwise would have kept shut due to the presence of a man, an ex-cop no less.

There was a "sold" sign across Crystal's "for sale" sign on her front lawn. I hid out until Morgan, Vivian, Anjelica, Lisa, and Margaret showed up. I didn't see Daniels drive up, so I assumed he'd spent the night with Crystal.

I moved around to the back of the house. I tried the back door. It was unlocked. I silently let myself in. It wasn't unusual to find an unlocked back door. There were so many private security companies patrolling the area, besides the fact that you have to go through the main gate and the security guy there. So a little breaking and entering was no biggie. I heard voices from the living room. One of them was a deep voice, so I was right about Daniels already being there.

The kitchen was nowhere to hide. Crystal had a lot of stuff already boxed up but the coffee maker was on, and I needed to move locations. I found a spot in a large linen closet. I quietly closed the door and realized I could only hear about every other sentence, depending on who was talking.

Daniels started out. He warned the women that the police were hot on their heels about the deaths of their husbands and the M.I.A. state Sheraton was in. There had been a lot of publicity about all of them. At first, the public was sweet and caring about first Vivian's, and then Crystal's husbands dying. But when Alphonse went, people started looking at Avalon and its inhabitants in a different way. Were they cursed? Or was there more going on? He reminded them he no longer carried a badge but he was still a cop in his heart, and anything they might say here could be held against them.

Margaret piped up and said, "That won't be necessary. We've got a whole new lead for you. The girls and I have put our heads together and come up with the perfect solution to your unsolved crimes."

Margaret had Shaun's full attention.

Lisa spoke next, "We have some paperwork you might be interested in."

I heard a shuffling of papers then a low whistle from Daniel. Whatever they'd given him, it was hot.

Daniels said they all needed to take this to the station. He had a few calls to make on the way.

I heard some moving of chairs, shuffling feet, and wine glasses taken to the kitchen. I waited until I heard the front door slam for the fifth time before I dared come out of my hiding place. I was so frustrated I hadn't heard what those papers were, but I damn well was going to find out. I raced out of the closet while dialing Zac's number on my cell at the same time. This was all too juicy not to share with him.

40

THEY WERE IN THEIR CARS AND pulling out of their driveways before I could scoot out Crystal's back door and down the street to my house to get a car. I was very careful not to be spotted. I'd had to leave a message for Zac. I couldn't tell him much since I didn't know where everyone was going, but I resolved to call him the minute we got to our mystery destination.

Lisa and Margaret's car was the last in the convoy and the easiest to follow. They had taken Mags' Rolls, and it wasn't hard to keep my eyes on it even though I had to follow a few cars behind.

As I was driving, I felt a sort of rush. I really was digging this kind of thing and seriously considered changing my major from poly sci to law enforcement. Yeah, Zac would be cool, married to a cop. Or maybe an FBI agent. *Whoa, slow down, Cass…let's just see how this plays out first.*

I figured out where we were heading about six blocks before we got there. I was surprised but then I wasn't. It was the police station. I texted Zac our location.

I waited in the back for Zac to show up, which he did in record time. He jumped out of his dad's truck, "What are we doing here?"

"I don't know. Let's go find out."

As we headed into the station, a woman cop at one of the front desks asked if she could help us. Just then, I saw the gaggle of Avalon women plus Daniels through the glass door of the captain's office.

I told the lady, "No thank you, we're with them." I pointed down the hall, then grabbed Zac and we rushed in. There would be no sneaking around this time, no spying. We marched right into the middle of what seemed to be a very heated discussion and shocked them all.

Vivian turned, "Cassidy? Zac? What are you two doing here?"

I was ready with an answer, "I'm tired of not knowing what's going on. I lost my dad. My friends lost their dads. I want to know what you all know and what the police know. I think I have a right."

I looked down at the captain's desk and saw that it was cluttered with papers. Just glancing at them upside down, I could tell each woman had thrown down her bank statements and a copy of her husband's will. What the hell was going on?

Anjelica went up to Zac, "You shouldn't be here."

Zac was miffed, "Why not?"

Just then, movement outside in the hallway caught my eye. I turned and was blown away to see Tommy and Dorothy being escorted down the corridor in handcuffs. Zac saw them too and rushed out of the office. "Mom? Dad? What the hell is going on? Have you been arrested? Why?"

Tommy couldn't even meet his son's gaze. He looked down at the carpet as a chagrined Dotty said, "You'll hear about it all later. It's nothing really. Just relax. We'll get it all straightened out in no time."

Zac whipped around to face the captain, "You don't think they murdered those guys? They were Dad's best friends!"

The captain was in no mood to answer questions. "Who the fuck is this kid?"

Tommy piped up, "He's my son."

That gut-punched the captain a little, and he apologized. Then, he explained that yes, he actually had linked Dotty and Tommy to the murders of Alphonse, Hudson, Jonathan, Carson, and even Sheraton. Even though they hadn't found the body yet, they were pretty sure someone else had used his passport to leave the country.

Zac was ready to punch the guy, Shaun had to hold him back.

Zac shouted, "They were his best friends. He couldn't hurt a fly. Neither could my mom. You've got the wrong people. Why would you even think they had anything to do with those deaths? You're saying my dad rigged Hudson's garage door, and enticed Jonathan to sleep with all those women, and stashed Sheraton's body somewhere, and shot up Carson with heroin?"

"Seems impossible, I know. And we don't have one shred of evidence to connect them to the crimes. But we've got plenty of other nasty shit on them. Hollister, take Mr. and Mrs. Nolan to the interrogation room while I sort all these papers out with these ladies." Hollister grabbed Dotty and Tommy. Zac was nearly in tears.

Tommy called back to his son, "It will be alright. We're innocent."

Zac wanted to follow his parents but Shaun shook his head, letting Zac know that was one place he couldn't go. And actually he and I needed to wait outside the captain's office for a while.

Shaun had a very tender look on his face for us. "I promise you, when we've got it all sorted out, I'll come out and tell you everything."

We had no choice but to go sit out on a very hard wooden bench outside the office. We couldn't hear what was being said but we could see each of the women, one at a time, go over the documents they'd brought with them, explaining things to the captain. That went on for over an hour. I squeezed Zac's hand and told him I loved him. But he was beyond comfort. He just sat there, shell-shocked, watching, and waiting.

Finally, the captain called one of the uniformed officers in. They had organized all the papers into one huge pile. The captain asked for the papers to be copied and to not screw up the order. The officer moved off, and Anjelica, Morgan, and Lisa came out of the office and over to us. They told us they loved us very much. They had taken a straw poll and decided it would be best if Detective Daniels explained everything to us. I said thank you. Zac just looked off into space.

Crystal and Vivian came out next. Vivian asked me if I wanted her to stay. I told her that was the last thing I wanted.

After Vivian and Crystal left, the captain got his copies and ordered the officer to make sure all the women got back all their originals. Then, the captain shot us an apologetic look and headed down the hall, obviously on his way to question Tommy and Dotty.

Daniels came out and said, "Come on, let's go across the street for a cup of coffee."

I rose to my feet. There was just something so kind and honest in his eyes. I could see why it took Crystal all of about twelve seconds to fall in love with the guy. I reached down for Zac's hand. He didn't move.

I leaned down and whispered in his ear. "We have to find out. Come on, honey, let's get this over with." He kind of snapped to and stood up.

The three of us went across the street to a lousy diner that served even lousier coffee. But we didn't care. We were there for information. Shaun took a sip and then launched into what he called a debriefing.

Zac demanded, "What led the cops to my parents?"

Daniels sipped his coffee, "It was really just a casual comment that Dotty made to Crystal at the party last night. She said she was appreciative of the forgiven debt in Jonathan's will and the extra money. The golfing buddies had always been generous with Tommy. Crystal worried as to what Tommy would do now for money. Dotty was sure Tommy's friends were more loyal than hers were. She knew that lately, she'd been left out in the cold, ostracized by the other women. She said something to the effect that Tommy's buddies would always be loyal—even in death.

That got Crystal thinking. What if Jonathan wasn't the only guy who was generous to Tommy? She called the girls together, and they looked at all the wills. When they had first read them with their lawyers, they were really focused only on what had been left to them. There were so many chunks of money they'd donated here and there and it really didn't seem like much went outside the family, so they never read the full will. They were shocked by just how generous their husbands had been with Tommy. Of course, money had meant nothing to them. But still, when they added it all up, all the wills specified that Tommy's debts would be forgiven to the total of over one million dollars. And they each left Tommy money on top of that. When they put all that together, they realized he was getting about two million dollars total bequeathed to him."

Daniels continued, "When there's a homicide, the first thing we do is look for who would profit the most. Anyone who knows your little group as well as you and I do, knows that the wives stood the most to gain. Not all of them got a windfall because of some tricky wording in their pre-nuptial agreements. Vivian inherited the company and a lot of Hudson's money, and Lisa got nothing. Morgan hasn't gotten anything because her husband hasn't yet been declared dead. But she has access to all his accounts and will certainly live a lush life. Anjelica got lucky. Alphonse was in the process of cutting her out of his will but he died first. That would make her a suspect, but she's got an airtight alibi for that night."

Zac was terse and accusatory. "You're going to profit from Crystal's money now that you're together."

"We don't want Jonathan's millions. Crystal gave every penny to charity including what she got for the house. Now we're broke and I'm out of work, but it will turn out alright. I couldn't stomach living on that dick's money."

Zac looked Shaun dead in the eyes. You could see there was a new-found respect Zac felt for Daniels. But there was still the bitter matter of his parents' arrest.

Daniels tried to make it clear, "Don't you see? Your dad gained millions. We know all that stuff about the wives but the captain doesn't, and I don't see any reason why he should. Even if he knew the wretched state of affairs in each of those marriages, those ladies will lawyer up in two seconds, and their attorneys would point out there isn't a speck of evidence against any of them. There isn't even enough to charge them. And things would have been cool with your parents too. But they got greedy."

Zac was still defensive, "It's not against the law to inherit money."

"No, if your dad had just stopped there. But he had been taking money from his buddies for so long, he felt entitled to it. He had become such a sponge—sorry, Zac—that he didn't know any other way to keep up the lifestyle he and Dorothy had become so accustomed to.

"And Crystal got a definite vibe last night from Dotty. Though she tried to cover it, Dot was royally pissed off. She knew something had been going on with the Ladies and she was feeling left out, like they all thought they were too good for her. But she kept her resentments to herself and every time she knew one of her pals was out of the house, she went in the back door and helped herself to some checks—a few at first, and small. But as time passed and she didn't get caught, she got bolder and took more and more. The women had no idea. They had never managed the family finances before and didn't check the numbers or the balance or anything. Dotty wrote checks to herself from all of them. Not enough to raise a red flag, but enough to stockpile her own stash. Between Tommy and Dotty, they amassed five million dollars. I have a friend who's a forensic accountant. He snooped around and found out your parents just bought a mansion just outside Vegas for 1.3 million dollars with cash. If they keep that up, they'll run out of money soon. But Tommy fancies himself a gambler and he feels like since all this money has just fallen into his lap, his luck will change.

"I'm sorry, Zac. This doesn't paint your parents in a very good light. The press will have a field day. Although we could never convict them on the murders, everyone will think they committed them. They are going to jail for grand theft. Public opinion will go against them. Things will be assumed. People will think it's sort of like getting Al Capone for tax fraud. I'm afraid they'll be labeled murderers for the rest of their lives."

Zac bit into his lower lip, "What kind of sentence will they get?"

Daniels shook his head, "I don't think it will be for very long, but you never know."

Zac pushed away his untouched coffee, "Can I see them?"

Shaun threw some money on the table and said, "Sure."

We got back to the station just as the captain was finishing up taking

Dotty and Tommy's statements. They were about to be separated when we walked in. I could tell that separation from each other was going to be the cruelest punishment of all.

Zac walked right up and threw his arms around them. "I love you, Mom. I love you too, Dad. I'll try to get a good attorney and get you out as soon as possible. You took me in when I needed a real family. You clothed me and fed me and loved me, and I'll always be grateful for that. But what you did was really wrong. You're going to have to pay for that."

Tommy and Dotty nodded, tears in both their eyes. After all three promised to call each other soon, Tommy and Dotty were taken away. Zac seemed stronger. He took my hand and held it up to his mouth and kissed it. Then he managed a half a smile and said, "Don't we have a plane to catch?"

CRYSTAL

January 20

EPILOGUE

I WAS SO NERVOUS I DECIDED to help myself to a glass of champagne. The hairdresser was taking forever, and I was growing impatient. I just wanted something simple. Elegant, of course, but simple.

I looked in the mirror to see the Ladies behind me running around like little bees. Anjelica was steaming my dress, and Morgan was laying out my veil and shoes. Vivian was calling room service, ordering more champagne, which was the last thing we really needed. I wanted all my best friends sober at my wedding.

Lisa pushed the hairdresser out of the way, "That's enough. Stop fussing, she looks just fine. I just want to add a tad more eyeliner…"

Lisa had her turn with me. As she was applying some lip gloss, Margaret came in, dressed to the nines with a matching cane, looking as regal as ever. "It's time to start, ladies."

I got up, and Morgan fixed my veil as I slipped into my shoes. The champagne just arrived as we were about to head out. Vivian was conscientious enough to have also ordered a bottle of sparkling cider for Lisa, who was obviously with child. Her stomach was enormous. She had gained fifty pounds during her pregnancy, but she didn't care. She was so happy and she rubbed her stomach, anxious to hold her little boy. I guess I should have been jealous but I wasn't. I was too in love with Shaun. We'd already begun the adoption process and were very at peace about it. When the right baby came along, we would know it. Meanwhile, we were just going to enjoy living together, loving each other, and going on a two-week honeymoon in Hawaii, a gift from the gals. Money wasn't much of a problem since Shaun started his own private investigation firm, but we still decided against an elaborate wedding. I'd already had one of those, and look how that turned out.

We were at the Venetian in Vegas, and I was just about to go downstairs and marry the man of my dreams. But Morgan insisted on a toast first. So we all went out to the balcony and looked at each other. It was such an emotional moment, no one knew what to say.

Finally, the sage amongst us, Margaret, told us to raise our glasses and she offered up this toast, "Here's to getting away with murder and living happily ever after."

❧

Just as our glasses clinked, back in Avalon, something floated to the surface of the lake. This was unusual as the owners made sure the lake was free of garbage all the time. But this wasn't a piece of garbage. It was a bloated, partially decomposed body...

ACKNOWLEDGMENTS

I WOULD SINCERELY LIKE TO THANK Kathy Edwards, Barry Felsen, Jeff Herman, Dana Higley, Greg Meng, Dick Roberts, Mike Russell, and Megan Trank for all of their help and guidance while I was writing this book.

Very special thanks to my wife, Sherry, and my children, Amanda, Kimberly, and Teddy, who continually show me that love is all you need.

Finally, as a point of clarification, the town of Avalon is a fictional place, and the *Ladies of the Lake* are fictional characters.